Martin Jacoby

Descriptions of the new genera and species of phytophagous

Coleoptera

Obtained by Mr. Andrewes in India

Martin Jacoby

Descriptions of the new genera and species of phytophagous Coleoptera
Obtained by Mr. Andrewes in India

ISBN/EAN: 9783741195792

Manufactured in Europe, USA, Canada, Australia, Japa

Cover: Foto ©Andreas Hilbeck / pixelio.de

Manufactured and distributed by brebook publishing software
(www.brebook.com)

Martin Jacoby

Descriptions of the new genera and species of phytophagous Coleoptera

DESCRIPTIONS OF THE NEW GENERA AND SPECIES OF

PHYTOPHAGOUS COLEOPTERA

OBTAINED BY Mr ANDREWES IN INDIA,

by Martin Jacoby.

PART. II. — *CHRYSOMELINÆ*, *HALTICINÆ* AND *GALERUCINÆ*.

CHRYSOMELINÆ.

Chrysomela bella Jac. (*C. cærulans*? Scrib.)

Metallic green varied with cupreous, antennæ blackish, thorax closely punctured, the sides variolose-punctate, cupreous as well as two central patches, elytra finely and semi-regularly punctate, the interstices partly aciculate, cupreous, the suture and a lateral longitudinal band purplish.

Length 2 1/2-3 lines.

Similar in shape to *C. graminis* or *C. fastuosa* of Europe and of the same system of coloration as several Alpine species of *Orina* but belonging I think to *Chrysomela* proper on account of the long first abdominal segment and other particulars, the head remotely but deeply punctured as well as the clypeus, cupreous, the vertex, a narrow central ridge and the space round the eyes shading into metallic green, labrum of the latter colour, apex of mandibles fulvous, antennæ comparatively long, extending beyond the base of the elytra, the lower five joints metallic green, the rest black, pubescent, third joint elongate, fourth and fifth equal, the following joints robust and thickened, but longer than broad, palpi robust, the third and fourth joint equal in lenght, thorax more than twice as broad as long, the sides very evenly and gradually rounded towards the apex, thickened, the thick portion preceded by large, deep and confluent punctures, the rest of the surface rather closely and finely but distinctly punctured, the basal margin especially crowded with punctures, the lateral margins and two longitudinal bands at the sides, cupreous, the intervening spaces, metallic green, scutellum broader than long, violaceous or purplish, elytra parallel, the apex rounded, the surface with rather regular rows of fine but distinct punctures, the rows separated at even intervalls, the interstices more or less aciculate, the suture narrowly as well as a more or less distinct broader longitudinal band at the sides, purplish, the rest of the disc cupreous, elytral epipleuræ broad, their inner margin near the apex with a fringe of very short hairs, underside and legs cupreous, varied with metallic green, tarsi broad, dark blue, the first abdominal segment longer than the metasternum, prosternum slightly longitudinally sulcate, the male organ, cylindrical, very strongly curved, gradually narrowed towards the apex, the latter itself truncate, the upper cavity confined to the apex bounded above by the straight anterior margin of t he upper surface.

Hab. Chamba, Dalhousie in the Himalayas, also Ishang (China).

I give here a renewed description of this species described by me in the Entomologist 1890. The Indian specimens do not seem to differ sufficiently from those from China which served mefor the type, and as is the case with most species of this genus, the tendency to variation in colour and sculpturing is great. In comparing the species carefully with *C. coerulans* Scrib. which is found also in Syria and Armenia I am now inclined to believe that the present insect is nothing but the variety *C. subfastuosa* Motsch. or var. *angelica* Reiche which seems to have therefore a very extended habitat. I am at all events unable to find distinctive characters for a specific separation from those varieties which at the time were not known to me.

Chrysomela aurata Suffr.

I refer specimens from Belgaum and Canara to this species, of which Suffrian has given a short diagnosis which applies however equally well to several other Indian species; in the Baly collection an Indian *Chrysomela* is labelled *C. aurata* with which the specimens before me agree as well as with Suffrian's diagnosis. The insect is of a somewhat narrow and posteriorly pointed shape, brownish aeneous, it resembles greatly *C. separata* Baly in the sculpturing, but the thorax is less transverse and its sides not so strongly rounded, the latter are likewise variolose-punctate but the disc is scarcely impressed with any punctures, the elytra are rather more finely punctured and the punctuation is more distinctly arranged in double rows, which are plainly visible below the middle, forming as usual four double rows; the male organ is cylindrical and strongly convex or curved, the apex rather suddenly constricted and truncate, the upper cavity elongate, extending almost as far as the middle, although getting gradually shallower.

Chrysomela Bonvouloirii Baly.

Aeneous, thorax variolose-punctate at the sides, the disc very sparingly but strongly punctured, elytra with four double rows of

deep foveolate punctures, the interstices smooth and impunctate.
Length 3 1/2 lines.

Of broadly subquadrate shape, of dark bronze colour, the head
with a few very fine punctures, irregularly distributed, the vertex
with a central longitudinal groove, the clypeus strongly separated
by a triangular groove, antennæ only extending to the base of the
elytra, the basal joint quadrately widened, stained with fulvous
below, the terminal five joints widened, scarcely longer than broad,
the last more elongate with a short conical extra joint at the apex;
thorax nearly three times broader than long, the sides straight at
the base, but slightly rounded and narrowed anteriorly, anterior
angles acute but not produced, the surface rather convex, strongly
metallic, the disc with a few deep punctures, irregularly placed,
they are rather more frequent and smaller near the anterior
margin, the sides deeply variolose and confluently punctured, thickened, scutellum broad, impunctate, elytra convex and broad, the apex
rather evenly rounded, with four double rows of deep round
punctures, the rows ill defined near the apex, not regularly placed
and a row of smaller punctures near the suture, the interstices here
and there with a few very fine punctures, underside coloured like
above, nearly impunctate, metallic, the sides of the breast closely
and strongly punctured, tarsi densely clothed with yellowish
pubescence beneath; the male organ long and curved, cylindrical,
the apical margin truncate, slightly widened, the anterior cavity
short and broad, narrowed posteriorly, the lateral edges of the
cavity acute.

Hab. Belgaum, Madura (Bombay and Madras presidences).

In general appearance and colour this species is not unlike the
European *C. Banksi*, the want of the deep thoracic lateral sulcus
separates however the present insect at once; *C. orientalis* Wied.
also resembles it but is described as 5 lines in length besides other
differences; *C. micans* Jac. is larger, of entirely different shape
and strongly deflexed posteriorly, the elytral punctures are larger
and more closely placed; I have given here a more detailed description of Baly's species, the type with which I have compared it, the
author calls the colour « cupreus » but dark æneous or bronze-
colour is a better definition of the tint.

PSEUDOLINA n. gen.

Subelongate-ovate, apterous, antennæ filiform, terminal joint
of palpi as long as the preceding one, truncate at the apex, thorax
transversely subquadrate, the sides nearly straight, scutellum
twice as broad as long, elytra widened at the middle, pointed

posteriorly, irregularly punctured, their epipleuræ broad, not furnished with hairs, legs rather slender, tibiæ dilated towards the apex, not channelled, the first joint of the posterior tarsi slightly longer than the following one, claws simple, prosternum narrow, elongate, mesosternum of somewhat similar shape, slightly raised posteriorly, metasternum scarcely longer than the prosternum, anterior coxal cavities closed.

The species for which I propose this genus resembles in its general shape and appearance certain Malayan forms of *Phyllocharis* or *Lamprolina*; the closed cavities and simple claws would place the genus near *Entomoscelis* and *Potaninia*, but the entirely different shape of the prosternum and mesosternum, the irregularly punctured elytra and want of wings prevent it of being included in that group.

Pseudolina indica n. sp.

Entirely metallic greenish or brownish æneous, the head finely punctured at the vertex, the eyes slightly kidneyshaped, the clypeus separated from the face, by a deep transverse groove, narrowly transverse, with a few fine punctures, antennæ nearly extending to the middle of the elytra in the male, black, the basal two joints more or less stained with fulvous, the first short and thick, scarcely longer than broad, the second one short, the third about one half longer than the fourth joint and as long as the fifth, thorax twice as broad as long, the sides nearly straight, not thickened, very slightly narrowed at the base, the posterior angles pointed, the anterior ones obtusely rounded, posterior margin straight, not marginate, the disc rather convex, finely, irregularly and rather closely punctured, scutellum narrowly transverse, its apex pointed, elytra widened at the middle, strongly pointed towards the apex, finely and irregularly punctured, the interstices here and there aciculate, prosternum finely rugose; the penis is very short and broad, of equal width. deeply chanelled at the undersurface, the apex furnished with a few bristles.

North Western Provinces.

Entomoscelis (*Potaninia*) assamensis Baly.

Specimens of this species, described by Weise as *Potaninia polita*, I possess from different parts of India and China; the species was originally described by Baly as *E. assamensis* from Assam but differs sufficiently from *Entomoscelis* I think, to justify its separation generically, but the name *polita* must sink as a synonym.

CHALCOLAMPRA 18-GUTTATA Fab.

A single specimen from Kanara; this species seems to be very
widely distributed. I possess specimens from Sumatra, Perak and
China. Weise, who apparently did not know the species, has
redescribed it as *Phola Keyserlingi*, at least, he does not compare
it with *Chalcolampra* and his description agrees entirely with the
present species.

HALTICINÆ.

HALTICA CYANEA Weber.

Dark blue, the antennæ black, thorax impunctate, the posterior
sulcus sinuate, elytra rather strongly and closely punctured.

Length 2 lines.

Head impunctate, frontal tubercles strongly raised, trigonate,
carina rather broad, antennæ extending nearly to the middle of
the elytra, black, the basal two joints dark fulvous at the apex,
the third joint double the lenght of the second but shorter than the
fourth; thorax twice as broad as long, the lateral margin slightly
rounded and produced at the middle, the disc entirely impunctate,
the basal sulcus sinuate, placed at some distance from the basal
margin, scutellum nearly black, broad, impunctate, elytra very
closely and rather strongly punctured, more finely so near the apex;
the penis elongate, of equal width, the apex rather broadly rounded, produced at the middle to a short truncate point, the underside smooth, with a longitudinal groove at each side near the apex.

Hab. Kanara, Belgaum, S. Bombay, Chamba (Himalayas).

I have given here a more detailed description of what I believe
to be the true *H. cyanea* of Weber which has evidently a very
wide geographical distribution; the short diagnosis published by
the author applies of course to a great number of species equally
well, which can perhaps be best distinguished by the shape of the
male organ; I have examined the latter in specimens from Java
and Sumatra and found it to agree entirely with those from the
Indian localities quoted above. The following species from Burmah
seems however to be distinct.

Haltica birmanensis n. sp.

Metallic bright blue, the antennæ black, thorax impunctate,
elytra with irregular rows of punctures, the interstices slightly
rugose, the sides with one or two longitudinal grooves.

Length 2 1/2 lines.

Of rather larger size than the preceding species, more brilliant lighter blue, the antennæ extending beyond the middle of the elytra, the latter with the punctures less closely placed and arranged in irregular rows, the sides with a longitudinal narrow depression at the middle, sometimes preceded by another less distinct one, the penis very nearly identical in shape with that of *II. cyanea.*

Hab. Burmah (my collection).

Although the penis of this species agrees with that of the preceding species, the sculpture of the elytra, the longer antennæ and brighter blue colour prevent me from looking upon it as a variety only, there are four specimens contained in my collection which agree entirely in the sculpturing of the elytra, no trace of a depression being visible in the numerous Indian and Sumatran specimens before me.

Some specimens from Chamba in the Himalayas, I have at present also referred to *H. cyanea,* as they only seem to differ in a finer elytral punctuation, the penis agrees however with that of the other males from India and Sumatra.

Aphthona kanaraensis n. sp.

Pale testaceous, terminal joints of the antennæ and the labrum, black, thorax impunctate, elytra microscopically punctured, the breast and the apex of the posterior femora more or less blackish.

Length 1 line.

Head impunctate, the frontal elevations in shape of narrow transverse ridges, carina short but distinctly raised, antennæ not extending to the middle of the elytra, flavous, the terminal six or seven joints black, third and fourth joints equal, scarcely longer than the second joint but thinner, terminal joints but slightly longer, thorax about one half broader than long, the sides straight, the anterior angles oblique, posterior margin slightly rounded, the surface entirely impunctate, posterior angles also oblique, scutellum small, obscure fuscous or pale, elytra wider at the base than the thorax, convex, exceedingly minutely and closely punctured, posterior femora more or less darkened at the apex, their tibiæ straight, widened posteriorly, armed with a spine near the outer edge, the first joint of the posterior tarsi as long as the following joints together, the tarsi slightly darkened, breast more or less black, the penis narrow and slender; the apex drawn out into a spine-like point.

Hab. Kanara.

Aphthona nigrilabris Duviv.

A few specimens from Belgaum agree well with a specimen kindly given to me by the author but the elytra have rows of extremely fine punctures, scarcely visible and placed at irregular distances; Duvivier speaks of some transparent (?) punctures placed in rows of four with smooth interstices : this was probably an exceptional condition of the elytra due to immaturity or other causes; in the specimen received by me, I am not able to see this arrangement of sculpturing; A. *nigrilabris* is more than double the size of the preceding species.

Aphthona Andrewesi n. sp.

Below bluish-black, above metallic dark blue, the basal joints of the antennæ flavous, thorax impunctate, elytra very finely and semi-regularly punctured.

Length 1/2 line.

Head impunctate, with a few punctures near the inner margins of the eyes, frontal tubercles very obsolete and small, limited behind by an oblique groove at each side, carina short, tuberculiform, labrum black, antennæ extending beyond the middle of the elytra, the terminal joints thickened, blackish, the lower four or five joints flavous, the basal joint stained with piceous above, second joint thickened, nearly as long as the third, the latter equal to the fourth joint; thorax about one half broader than long, the sides moderately rounded, the anterior angles oblique, the surface impunctate, metallic dark blue, scutellum triangular, black, elytra finely punctured in closely approached semi-regular rows, which become rather obsolete at the apex; legs more or less piceous, the tibiæ rather paler, the metatarsus of the posterior legs as long as the following joints together; prosternum very narrow.

Hab. Chamba, Himalayas.

A very small species, principally distinguished on that account from several other Eastern forms, also by the impunctate thorax and darkly coloured legs.

Aphthona azurea n. sp.

Broadly ovate, short, entirely metallic bright blue, antennæ, tibiæ and tarsi black, head and thorax impunctate, elytra extremely finely punctured, the apex nearly impunctate.

Length 1 line.

Head impunctate, eyes large, frontal elevations narrowly oblique, the clypeus with an acutely raised central ridge, antennæ robust, extending beyond the middle of the elytra, black, the third and fourth joint equal, the following joints thickened but distinctly longer than broad, thorax twice as broad as long, the sides nearly straight, narrowly margined, the anterior angles oblique, forming a distinct tooth or angle before the middle, posterior margin broadly rounded, but slightly produced at the middle, the surface entirely impunctate, even when seen under a strong lens, scutellum broader than long, black, elytra wider at the base than the thorax, slightly widened at the middle with a narrow margin, finely and semiregularly punctured, the apex impunctate, breast and abdomen black with a slight bluish tint, the legs more distinctly metallic blue, the metatarsus of the posterior legs as long as the following joints together, the penis rather long and slender, not strongly curved, the apex slightly widened into a triangular point, the upper cavity long and extending nearly to the middle.

Hab. Burmah.

A small species of a pretty metallic blue colour, which may be known by the similarly coloured legs and the entirely impunctate thorax; wings are present.

Phyllotreta flaviventris n. sp.

Black, thorax fulvous, minutely punctured, elytra closely and more strongly punctured, black, abdomen flavous.

Length 1 1/4 line.

Of elongate and parallel shape, the head black, impunctate, the frontal tubercles small, trigonate, the carina strongly raised, not very sharp, palpi piceous, the terminal joint acute, antennæ nearly extending to the middle of the elytra, black, the lower joints slightly marked with fulvous below, second and third joint short, equal, fourth rather longer than the following joint, thorax one half broader than long, the sides slightly rounded and gradually narrowed anteriorly, the posterior angles strongly oblique, the anterior ones slightly produced and thickened, the surface rather flattened, extremely minutely punctured, fulvous, scutellum black, smooth, elytra wider at the base than the thorax, closely, finely but distinctly punctured; the anterior legs more or less stained with fulvous, posterior femora very strongly incrassate, black as well as their tibiae, the latter with a distinct spur; abdomen entirely or partly flavous.

Hab. Belgaum, S. Bombay.

Phyllotreta bombayensis n. sp.

Pale fulvous or testaceous, the antennæ, breast and the legs more or less black, thorax impunctate, elytra scarcely perceptibly punctured, testaceous, the sutural and lateral margins and the apex black.

Var. The underside and legs as well as the elytral margins obscure fulvous.

Length 1 1/2 line.

Head impunctate, the frontal tubercles obsolete, clypeus with a distinct central ridge, labrum piceous, antennæ rather robust, black, the lower two joints more or less obscure fulvous, second joint thickened not shorter than the third, fourth and fifth more elongate, rather stout as well as the following slightly shorter joints, thorax one half broader than long, the lateral margins very slightly rounded, posterior angles obliquely rounded, anterior ones obsolete, the disc with a very obscure depression at the sides, impunctate, fulvous, scutellum black, elytra extremely minutely punctured, the margins blackish, the pale portion forming a broad, medially narrowed longitudinal band, legs blackish, the anterior ones and the tibiæ partly stained with fulvous, abdomen flavous, the apex darker.

Hab. Belgaum, Dharwar, S. Bombay.

The design of the elytra in the plainly marked form resembles much that of several European species in which the elytra are marked by a more or less distinct straight or curved pale vitta; *P. birmanica* Har. seems another closely allied species but differs entirely in the sculpture of the thorax and of the elytra. I am not able to say anything about the sexes of the present species, as all the specimens I have examined proved to be females.

PHYLLOTRETA CHOTANICA Duv.

I refer some specimens from Belgaum to this species, as they agree well with the author's description, the colour of the four specimens obtained is dark blue and the punctuation of the thorax and the elytra very distinct.

Longitarsus madurensis n. sp.

Below piceous, above flavous, labrum black, thorax finely and closely punctured, elytra punctured like the thorax, the suture narrowly black, posterior femora piceous.

Length 3/4 line.

Head obscure piceous or dark fulvous, with a row of distinct punctures placed transversely between the eyes, clypeus with an acute and long central ridge, blackish as well as the labrum, antennæ extending to the middle of the elytra, fulvous, the terminal joints darker, basal joint rather long, the second one scarcely shorter than the third joint, terminal joints thickened, thorax one half broader than long, the sides rather strongly rounded, the

angles not prominent, the surface rather convex, finely and closely
punctured, the punctures slightly elongate in shape, scutellum
broader than long, elytra widened towards the middle, as closely
punctured as the thorax, but the punctures rather larger, the apex
of each elytron separately rounded, underside and the posterior
femora more or less blackish or piceous as well as the pygidium,
the metatarsus of the posterior legs half the length of the tibia.

Hab. Madura, Madras Presidency.

This species belongs to a group in which the suture of the elytra
is narrowly black, to distinguish it from others, similarly coloured,
the punctation of the space between the eyes, the dark labrum and
underside as well as the close punctuation of the thorax and elytra
must be taken into consideration; it is also closely allied to *L. birmanicus* Jac., but that species has a more transversely shaped
and finely punctured thorax, longer antennæ, fulvous labrum and
other differences.

Longitarsus nigronotatus n. sp.

Pale fulvous, the apical joints of the antennæ piceous, thorax
transverse, finely punctured and distinctly transversely sulcate,
elytra finely and semi-regularly punctured, a round spot at the
middle, the apex and the suture posteriorly, black.

Length 3/4 line.

Head impunctate, the frontal elevations small, nearly joined to
the clypeus which is strongly convex and impunctate, eyes large,
the space dividing them narrower than their diameter, antennæ
robust, black, the lower four joints fulvous, second joint half the
length of the first, third and fourth small, equal, following joints
thickened and elongate, thorax nearly twice as broad as long, the
sides straight, the anterior angles obliquely truncate, the base with
a distinct, slightly sinuate sulcation, the surface finely and
sparingly punctured, more closely so below the sulcation, elytra
with fine punctures, placed in irregular rows, each with a rather
large round spot, placed at the middle, the apex, and the suture
posteriorly, black, underside and legs fulvous, the apex of the
posterior femora with a small black spot, the metatarsus of the
posterior legs but little longer than the following joints together.

Hab. Tharrawaddy, Burmah.

L. nigronotatus, although closely allied in coloration to *L. bino-
tatus* Baly from Shanghai, differs in several particulars, the joints
of the antennæ are of proportionately different length, the transverse sulcation of the thorax is much more distinct and altogether
rather exceptional in this genus, and lastly, the elytra have an

extra spot at the apex, connected with the similarly coloured black suture at the posterior portion, of this however, there is in some specimens only a trace, as the black markings differ in size.

Longitarsus rufipennis n. sp.

Ovate, dark fulvous or rufous, antennæ as long as the body, black (the basal joints excepted); thorax broader than long, impunctate, elytra widened at the middle, nearly impunctate; legs black, base of femora and tibiæ fulvous.

Lenght 1 line.

Head impunctate, frontal elevations only indicated, carina acutely raised, palpi piceous, antennæ nearly extending to the end of the elytra, black, the lower three joints rufous, third joint one half shorter than the fourth, but longer than the second joint, the following ones elongate, thorax scarcely one half broader than long, the sides feebly rounded at the middle, the anterior angles oblique, the surface impunctate, scutellum broader than long, elytra widened towards the middle, the surface scarcely perceptibly punctured, wings absent, legs long and stout, black, the extreme base of the femora, fulvous, metatarsus of the posterior legs less than half the lenght of the tibia, the second joint half the lenght of the first, prosternum very narrow.

Hab. Madura, Madras Presidency.

Longitarsus belgaumensis n. sp.

Obscure fulvous, antennæ nearly as long as the elytra, labrum black, thorax subquadrate, nearly impunctate as well as the elytra, the suture very narrowly piceous, posterior femora black at the apex.

Length 1 line.

Of elongate and parallel shape, the head impunctate, without frontal elevations, clypeus with a central ridge, labrum black, antennæ not quite extending to the apex of the elytra, fulvous, the apical joints darker, second joint rather long, third slightly longer but shorter than the fourth joint, following ones elongate and slender, thorax one half broader than long, the sides slightly rounded near the base, the anterior angles greatly oblique, forming a tooth at a little distance before the middle, surface impunctate, but very finely wrinkled near the base, elytra subcylindrical, the suture very narrowly darker, the surface not perceptibly punctured, posterior femora very long and thick, their apex black, penis very straight and slender, slightly narrowed at some distance from the apex, the latter pointed.

Hab. Belgaum.

Differs from *L. birmanicus* Jac. in not having the head and the scutellum dark and in the impunctate elytra and shorter antennæ.

Oedionychys inornata n. sp.

Obscure pale fulvous or testaceous, the thorax with flattened sides, impunctate; elytra extremely finely and closely punctured; posterior claw-joints piceous.

Length 3 ¹/₂-4 lines.

Of nearly parallel and rather depressed shape, the head impunctate, the space separating the eyes, slightly wider than their diameter, frontal tubercles small, but slightly raised, clypeus very short, transversely raised, antennæ not extending to the middle of the elytra, pale, the lower two joints darker and shining, the third and fourth equal, thorax more than twice as broad as long, the sides moderately rounded with a rather broad, flattened margin, the anterior angles very slightly produced and thickened, posterior margin straight, the surface entirely impunctate, scutellum triangular, elytra extremely minutely and finely punctured, their epipleuræ broad, concave, underside finely and sparingly pubescent, posterior femora strongly incrassate, the first joint of the posterior tarsi scarcely longer than the second one, posterior claws strongly inflated, piceous, prosternum narrow, not sulcate.

Hab. Belgaum, S. Bombay.

I have placed this species in *Oedionychis* on account of the short metatarsus of the posterior legs which agrees better with this genus than with *Hyphasis*, the latter genus being further distinguished by the extremely broad elytral epipleuræ. There is however one difference in the present insect as well as in several other Eastern species, at present included in *Oedionychis*, that is the absence of the emargination of the posterior tibiæ at the apex which is present in all the true Southern species of *Oedionychis*, although this character may be subject to modification and in itself is not sufficient for a generic separation. *O. inornata* may easily be mistaken for *Hyphasis indica* Baly which it resembles entirely in coloration, but the structure of the head and that of the posterior tarsi are quite different and will at once separate the two species.

Oedionychis japonicus Baly.

Specimens of this species, originally described by Baly from Nagasaki in Japan, were obtained by Mʳ Andrewes at Belgaum; I cannot find any differences to justify a separation from Japanese specimens in my collection.

Hyphasis discoidalis n. sp.

Pale fulvous, thorax impunctate, elytra finely and closely punctured, the disc obscure fulvous, the margins obscure piceous.
Length 1 1/2 line.

Of ovate shape, the head impunctate, the frontal elevations
transverse, rather flat, carina short but distinct, clypeus deflexed,
antennæ extending to the middle of the elytra, flavous, the
terminal joints fuscous, third and following joints equal, elongate,
thorax transverse, nearly three times broader than long, the sides
slightly rounded, the posterior margin somewhat broadly produced
at the middle, anterior angles blunt, the surface impunctate, pale
flavous, scutellum triangular, flavous, elytra very closely, finely
but distinctly punctured, all the margins narrowly obscure piceous,
the disc obscure fulvous, their epipleuræ deeply concave, prosternum narrowly elongate.

Hab. Belgaum, S. Bombay.

The two specimens before me agree in everything, except that
in one, the elytra are darker fulvous than in the other, both
colours being very obscure.

Hyphasis tenuilimbatus n. sp.

Testaceous, the antennæ (the basal joints excepted) black, thorax
impunctate, elytra very closely and finely punctured, very narrowly
margined with black.

Length 2 lines.

Head impunctate, eyes large, frontal elevations strongly raised,
trigonate, carina short and blunt, clypeus deflexed, antennæ
extending to the middle of the elytra, black, the lower three joints
testaceous, third joint one half shorter than the fourth; thorax
transverse, more than twice as broad as long, the sides evenly
rounded, with a narrow reflexed margin, the anterior angles
thickened and slightly produced outwards, the surface rather
convex, impunctate, shining, elytra parallel, finely and closely
punctured, all the margins very narrowly black, their epipleuræ
deeply concave, posterior femora greatly dilated, the first joint of
the posterior tarsi as long as the following two joints together,
claw-joint swollen.

Hab. Kanara, S. Bombay.

Hyphasis thoracica n. sp.

Black, the head and thorax flavous, the former with one, the
latter with four black spots, elytra finely punctured, chestnutbrown.
Length 2 lines.

Of broadly ovate and convex shape, the head impunctate, the vertex with a black spot, frontal elevations narrowly transverse, carina acutely raised, lower portion of face rather elongate, flavous, the clypeus broad, penultimate joint of the palpi, incrassate, terminal joint acute, antennæ extending to the middle of the elytra, black, the lower two joints obscure fulvous, basal joint elongate, second one, one half shorter than the third, the latter slightly shorter than the fourth and following joints, thorax three times broader than long, flavous, the sides strongly rounded, with a narrow flattened margin, anterior angles thickened, the surface sparingly and finely punctured, with four round black spots, placed transversely at equal distances, the two middle ones higher than those at the sides, scutellum very broad, flavous, triangular, elytra convex, reddish-brown, very finely but not very closely punctured, their epipleuræ flavous, underside and legs black, the first joint of the posterior tarsi, longer than the following two joints, claw-joint strongly swollen, tibiæ deeply chanelled.

Hab. Belgaum.

ARGOPISTES LIMBATUS? Motsch.

I refer some specimens from Belgaum to this species, although it would have been perfectly justifiable to describe them as new, as Motschulsky's description of two lines is entirely useless; the shape of the insect is that of a small *Coccinella*, the antennæ, underside and legs are fulvous, the head above, the thorax and elytra are black with a very narrow fulvous margin, which agrees with the author's description; the head is sometimes fulvous and the sides are entirely occupied by the very large eyes which are divided by a very narrow space only, the clypeus formes as usual in this genus a highly raised triangular ridge, the sides being deeply concave, the antennæ do not reach to the middle of the elytra and are rather slender, the terminal joints are scarcely thickened, the basal one is long, the three following joints are short and the others slightly more elongate, the thorax agrees in shape with the other species of the genus and is, like the elytra very finely and closely punctured, the elytral epipleuræ have their inner margins placed deeply within, posterior femora strongly dilated, their tibiæ short, widened and sulcate, the apex produced laterally and provided at the middle with a strong spur, the metatarsus is as long as the following joints together; metasternum with an elongate boat-shaped smooth depression, the first abdominal segment scarcely longer than others; prosternum longer than broad; the length of the specimens is 1 1/2 line.

It is of course possible, that the present species is specifically

distinct from Motschulsky's who described his type from the
Amur river but the coloration at all events is identical.

Argopistes laevigata n. sp.

Subhemispherical, fulvous, the thorax with two, the elytra with
three small spots placed triangularly, the upper surface impunctate.

Var. Thorax and elytra without spots.

Length 2 lines.

Head impunctate, the eyes elongate, large, clypeus raised into
an acute triangular ridge, penultimate joint of the palpi incrassate,
antennæ extending slightly beyond the thorax, entirely fulvous,
the first joint very long and slender, the second thickened, short,
the following three joints equal, terminal joints thickened, scarcely
longer than broad, the last one longer ; thorax strongly curved,
the sides oblique, the anterior angles thickened, the anterior
margin deeply concave at the sides, nearly straight at the middle.
posterior margin strongly curved and oblique at the sides, the
latter sinuate, produced into a short lobe in front of the scutellum,
the surface impunctate, fulvous, with a round black spot at each
side of the base, scutellum small, triangular, elytra strongly
rounded, impunctate, two spots placed transversely before the
middle and another near the apex and intermediate between the
others, black, underside and legs coloured like the upper surface,
tibiæ triangularly widened, posterior femora strongly incrassate,
their tibiæ with a short spur, clothed with yellowish pubescence,
prosternum elongate.

Hab. Kanara.

At first sight, this species is identical with *A. bistripunctata*
Duv. likewise from India, the colour and the presence of the three
elytral black spots is the same, but the antennæ only extend to
the base of the elytra (not half the length of the body as Duvivier
describes his species) and the entire upper surface is without
punctures or the latter are so fine as to be practically called, absent ;
the thorax has also two large round spots (although the variety is
spotless) there is no trace of a double row of punctures at the
elytra or at the sides of the thorax. Weise has separated the
species of Duvivier from *Argopistes* and placed it in his genus
Chilocoristes, if rightly or wrongly I am not in a position to say,
but I see no reason to separate the present insect, it is easy
to multiply the genera to any extend in the exotic species, if every
little difference is thought of generic importance. In the insect
before me I see neither hairs at the side of the thorax nor a
tuberculous setæ at the posterior margin of the same part of which
Weise speaks.

Sphaeroderma flavoplagiata n. sp.

Subhaemispherical, dark fulvous, antennæ (the basal joints excepted) black, thorax finely punctured, elytra strongly punctate-striate, the interstices finely punctured, piceous, a large subtriangular patch from the base to the middle, flavous.

Length 2 lines.

Very convex, slightly narrowed posteriorly, the head impunctate, fulvous, the eyes very large, occupying the entire sides, frontal tubercles rather small, clypeus deflexed, its anterior edge straight, antennæ extending slightly beyond the base of the elytra, black, the lower three joints fulvous, the basal joint rather elongate, the second and third joint equal, short, the rest more elongate, nearly equal, thorax twice as broad as long, strongly widened at the middle, the sides slightly rounded, with a narrow reflexed margin, anterior angles obliquely rounded, posterior margin sinuate at the sides, its median lobe broadly rounded and produced, the surface very minutely punctured, the punctures nearly obsolete anteriorly, more distinct and larger near the base, scutellum fulvous, elytra regularly and strongly punctate-striate, the interstices everywhere finely punctured, the colour piceous, interrupted by a large pale flavous patch, which occupies the entire anterior half, extending below the middle, but not touching either margins, towards the sides the patch is gradually narrowed, tibiæ rather deeply chanelled, prosternum broad, subquadrate.

Hab. Toungoo.

The large flavous elytral patch principally distinguishes this species, the elytral epipleuræ are deeply concave and also flavous; *S. ornata* Baly has differently coloured antennæ and two elytral flavous spots on each. *Argopus Fortunei* Baly also resembles the present species but is larger, the clypeus is rugose, the antennæ are longer and the sculpturing of the elytra, as well as their colour, is different.

Erystus(?) indicus n. sp.

Fulvous, the breast and the abdomen piceous, head and thorax impunctate, elytra extremely finely and closely punctured, nearly black.

Length 1 line.

Head broader than long, the frontal elevations and the carina entirely obsolete, clypeus narrowly raised, transverse, palpi as well as the labrum fulvous, antennæ extending to the middle of the elytra, rather robust, fulvous, the terminal four joints black, basal joint rather long and thick, the following three joints equal, short, the others rather thickened, terminal joints more elongate, thorax twice as broad as long, the sides rather strongly rounded, the posterior margin to a smaller degree so, the angles not prominent, the base with a very narrow margin, the surface entirely impunctate, fulvous, scutellum black, elytra slightly wider than the thorax, extremely minutely punctured, the interstices very finely granulate when seen under a strong lens, blackish, their epipleuræ broad, continued to the apex, legs fulvous, the posterior tibiæ with a minute spine, posterior femora strongly incrassate, prosternum narrowly elongate, the anterior coxal cavities closed, first abdominal segment double the length of the second one.

Hab. Belgaum, S. Bombay.

Although this small species possesses most of the structural characters of the genus, it ought perhaps find its place in another one, and I have only placed it at present in *Erystus* till other species may turn up ; the shape is neither so broadly ovate as in the typical form nor are the elytra punctate-striate or costate, but in other respect the structural characters are the same ; it is a very small insect and may be known by the transverse thorax and its rounded sides.

Manobia dorsalis n. sp.

Black, the antennæ and legs fulvous, thorax impunctate, with a deep transverse sulcus, elytra punctate-striate, fulvous, the disc occupied by a broad bluish-black band.

Var Head fulvous, the discoidal elytral band nearly obsolete. Length 1 line.

Head impunctate, black or piceous, distinctly obliquely grooved between the eyes, antennæ extending to the middle of the elytra, fulvous, the second and third joints equal, the following joints slightly longer and gradually thickened, thorax one half broader than long, the sides straight. the anterior angles oblique, the disc with a transverse deep sinuate sulcus near the base, impunctate, fulvous, elytra with the basal portion swollen, strongly punctate-striate, the punctures obsolete at the apex, the latter and the sides fulvous, the rest of the disc occupied by a broad posteriorly narrowed bluish-black band, legs fulvous, underside black.

Hab. Madura (Madras Presidency).

Whether this species is really distinct from some very closely allied Malayan forms or not, I am somewhat in doubt, since all the species seem subject to great variation, but I know no other in which the elytra show the broad bluish-black band of the present insect, that is, where it is well marked, in the variety there is sometimes only a trace of it, the posterior femora have often a dark spot near the apex.

Pseudodera metallica n. sp.

Metallic green, the antennæ, tibiæ and tarsi flavous, thorax
finely punctured, with a deep transverse groove, elytra punctate-
striate, the basal portion raised.

Length 2 3/4-3 lines.

Of elongate and parallel shape, bright metallic green, the
vertex of the head impunctate with a deep oblique groove at each
side above the base of the antennæ, frontal tubercles rather small,
trigonate, carina acutely raised and long, the clypeus rugose, the
labrum black, margined with fulvous and impressed with a row
of deep punctures, antennæ extending beyond the middle of the
elytra, flavous, the second joint proportionately long, one half the
size of the third, the fourth nearly as long as the preceding, the
terminal joints slightly thickened; thorax twice as broad as long,
the sides very slightly rounded, very narrowly margined, the
anterior angles mucronate, the surface finely and rather closely
punctured, with a deep transverse groove near the base bounded
at each side by a perpendicular groove, scutellum rather small;
elytra wider at the base than the thorax, the base distinctly
swollen, the disc regularly punctate-striate, each elytron with
ten rows of punctures, rather obsolete near the apex, the latter
subtruncate, the interstices smooth; the underside rather more
cupreous in colour, less metallic; all the tibiæ mucronate, flavous,
the first joint of the posterior tarsi as long as the following joints
together, claws appendiculate, anterior coxal cavities closed;
posterior femora rather strongly incrassate.

Hab. Madura (Madras).

Although in this handsome species the antennæ are not tapering towards the apex as in the typical form and the metatarsus
of the posterior legs is longer, the general shape, structure of the
thorax agrees with *Pseudodera* of wich genus two species are
known, both inhabitants of the East. Although Baly made no
mention of any spines, I find that all the tibiæ in the typical form
are armed although the spine is very short and difficult to detect
at the anterior legs, in the present species they are however
very distinct.

Nisotra madurensis n. sp.

Rounded, convex, black, the head, base of the antennæ, thorax
and legs fulvous, elytra dark blue, minutely and closely punctured.

Length 1 1/2-2 lines.

Head impunctate without distinct frontal elevations, the clypeus
rather broad, scarcely separated, antennæ extending below the

base of the elytra black, the lower four joints fulvous, third and fourth and fifth joint slender, equal, the others rather shorter and thicker, thorax more than twice as broad as long, the sides rather strongly rounded before the middle, straight at the base, the anterior angles produced obliquely outwards, the anterior margin with a very deep and short perpendicular groove at each side, the surface scarcely perceptibly and rather sparingly punctured, fulvous, posterior margin entire, broadly produced at the middle, scutellum fulvous, elytra strongly rounded, convex, dark blue, very finely and closely punctured, the punctures near the lateral margin sowewhat regularly arranged in rows, epipleuræ very broad, transversely wrinkled, legs and prosternum fulvous, breast and abdomen black.

Hab. Madura, Madras Presidency.

I must separate this species from *N. Bowringi* Baly on account of the entirely irregular punctuation of the elytra and its general more rounded shape.

Podagrica (*Nisotra*) striatipennis n. sp.

Fulvous, thorax closely and very finely punctured, the anterior and posterior margin with two longitudinal grooves, elytra metallic blue, strongly punctate-striate, the interstices finely punctured, the breast black.

Length 1 1/2 line.

Of posteriorly pointed shape, the head fulvous, impunctate, the frontal tubercles rather obsolete, clypeus transversely raised, antennæ extending to the base of the elytra, robust, fulvous, the sixth to the tenth joint, black, thorax strongly transverse, more than twice as broad as long, the sides much rounded, the anterior angles thickened, the posterior margin slightly sinuate at the sides, the medial lobe but little produced and rounded, its sides with a deep but short perpendicular groove, similar grooves are placed at the sides of the anterior margin behind the eyes, the surface rather convex, very finely and rather closely punctured, scutellum fulvous, elytra nearly parallel, pointed at the apex, very strongly and rather regularly punctate-striate, each elytron having about ten rows of punctures, the interstices finely and closely punctured, legs fulvous, robust, the breast and the abdomen (the last segment excepted) more or less black.

Hab. Belgaum.

A very distinct species on account of the strong and regular elytral punctuation, the strongly rounded sides of the thorax and the colour of the antennæ. It is perhaps as well to unite *Nisotra* with *Podagrica* as Weise has suggested, since the only difference seems to be the anterior perpendicular grooves of the thorax in *Nisotra* which as a rule are absent in *Podagrica*.

Mantura indica n. sp.

Fulvous, above greenish-æneous, thorax very closely covered with larger and smaller punctures, without basal grooves, elytra distinctly punctate-striate, the interstices very closely and finely punctured.

Length 1 1/2 line.

Of elongate and parallel shape, the head finely and closely punctured and minutely granulate, greenish-æneous, the clypeus and the labrum fulvous, frontal tubercles and carina absent, antennæ widely separated, inserted near the lower portion of the eyes, fulvous, extending slightly beyond the base of the thorax, the basal joint elongate, the second and third equal, the following joints slightly longer, thorax nearly three times broader than long, widened at the middle, the sides slightly rounded and narrowed in front, narrowly margined, the anterior angles pro- duced into a slightly truncate tooth, the surface closely impressed with round larger and numerous smaller punctures, crowded together, the larger punctures more numerous at the sides than at the middle, posterior margin broadly rounded and produced at the middle, scutellum triangular, elytra regularly and strongly punctate-striate, each elytra, with ten rows of punctures inclu- ding the short subsutural row, the interstices very closely and finely punctured; underside and legs fulvous, anterior coxal cavities closed.

Hab. Belgaum, South Bombay.

In this species the antennæ are more widely separated than is the case in its European allies and the thoracic perpendicular grooves at the base, found in some species are absent, but no other differences seem to be present, the general colour of the insect above is a dull greenish-æneous, caused by the dense and close punctuation.

Psylliodes tenebrosus n. sp.

Below black, above brownish-æneous, the base of the antennæ, the knees, apex of the tibiæ and the posterior tibiæ and tarsi fulvous.

Length 1 line.

Head distinctly and rather closely punctured, the frontal tubercles absent, the clypeus impunctate, antennæ extending to the middle of the elytra, black, the lower three joints flavous, the second and third joint, equal, elongate, fourth slightly longer, thorax one half broader than long, the sides straight, the anterior angles oblique, forming a distinct tooth before the middle, the disc punctured like the head, elytra strongly and very regularly punctate-striate, the rows closely placed, the interstices also closely and very finely punctured, underside und legs black, shining, the extreme base of the femora, the apex of the tibiæ, the posterior tibiæ entirely and their tarsi, fulvous.

Hab. Chamba, Himalayas.

Of narrowly elongate and parallel shape, of a dark æneous colour and in this respect dissimilar from most of its metallic blue congeners.

Chaetocnema geniculata n. sp.

Black, the apex of the femora and the tibiæ flavous, terminal joints of antennæ, black, thorax transverse, extremely finely and rather sparingly punctured, elytra deeply punctate-striate, the interstices flat and impunctate.

Length 1/2 line.

Of shining black colour, the head impunctate, with the exception of a single deep puncture at the inner margin of the eyes, frontal elevations absent, clypeus slightly raised between the antennæ, lower portion finely pubescent, impunctate, palpi flavous, antennæ slender, extending beyond the middle of the elytra, black, the lower four joints flavous, third and fourth joints equal, much longer than the second one, thorax twice as broad as long, the sides slightly rounded, the angles distinct, the posterior margin slightly produced at the middle and rounded, preceded by a row of small punctures, rest of the surface very minutely and not closely punctured, elytra broad at the base, narrowed posteriorly, strongly punctate-striate, the punctures round, larger than the space between each at the two first rows near the suture, the others more widely separated, those near the apex, smaller, interstices flat and impunctate, except the one near the lateral margin which is raised, elytral epipleuræ with a few punctures posteriorly, underside black and impunctate, the extreme apex of the femora and the tibiæ and tarsi, flavous, posterior tibiæ widened, distinctly notched at the middle, the first joint of the posterior tarsi as long as the following two joints.

Hab. Burmah.

This little species may be known by the impunctate head, the black shining colour of the upper and underside, the long and slender antennæ, flat elytral interstices and the colour of the legs.

Chaetocnema minuta n. sp.

Obscure æneous, head impunctate, thorax extremely finely and closely punctured, elytra strongly punctate-striate, the interstices minutely punctured, anterior legs and posterior tibiæ more or less flavous.

Length 1/2 line.

Head minutely granulose, with a few very fine punctures between the eyes, frontal elevations absent, antennæ black, the basal five or six joints fulvous, the second and the following two joints small and equal, thorax scarcely twice as broad as long, the sides nearly straight, gradually narrowed in front, the anterior angles scarcely oblique, the usual seta placed much below the angles, the surface extremely minutely and closely punctured, the interstices finely granulate, elytra moderately strongly punctate-striate, the punctures very closely placed within the striæ, the short sutural row as regular as the others, the interstices extremely minutely punctured, only visible under a strong lens, slightly costate at the sides, elytral epipleuræ impunctate, underside and femora obscure æneous, the anterior legs and the posterior tibiæ more or less flavous, strongly notched below the middle, with a long spine, their metatarsus as long as the following joints together; penis long and slender, gradually tapering towards the apex, the latter pointed.

Hab. Belgaum.

A very small species, which may be known from other Indian forms by the impunctate head, the very finely and closely punctured thorax, in connection with the finely punctured elytral interstices.

GALERUCINÆ.

Haplosoma Jac.

Several species belonging to this genus are not at all well defined and Allard, who has given a list of them has made several mistakes; his *H. corniculata* seems identical with *H. ventralis* Baly (Trans. Ent. Soc. Lond. 1886) which Allard does not mention, although Baly published his description two years before that of Allard. *H. unicolor* Illig. does not belong to *Haplosoma* but enters the genus *Haplosomoides* Duviv. on account of the appendiculate claws. *H. lunata* Redt. (*cyanura* Hope) likewise is no *Haplosoma* but belongs to *Mimastra*. In his synoptic list of the species, Allard gives one division, in which the breast and all the other portions are fulvous and the abdomen black, but he quotes no species belonging to this division, a species so coloured is however evidently peculiar to India and I give here the description of it.

Haplosoma abdominalis n. sp.

Elongate, testaceous or pale fulvous, abdomen black only, elytra rather distinctly and closely punctured, shining.

♂. Abdomen with two fulvous appendages, extending to the third segment.

Length 3 lines.

Head impunctate, frontal tubercles strongly raised, subquadrate, clypeus transversely elevated, antennæ extending to the middle of the elytra, fulvous, third joint shorter than the fourth, thorax one half broader than long, the sides slightly narrowed and concave posteriorly, the surface transversely sulcate, impunctate, elytra finely and closely punctured, shining, the shoulders prominent, the disc without depressions or costæ, abdomen black, the last segment of the male deeply incised at the sides, the median lobe flat.

Hab. Rangoon, also Cashar and Tenasserim.

The only species, with which the present one can be compared, are those in which the underside is black (*H. ventralis* Baly and *H. picefemora* Alld.) but in these species, the breast is black as well as the abdomen and in one or two others in which the underside is likewise black, the elytra have a longitudinal sulcation below the shoulders; in the present insect, the male organ is long and tapering, strongly curved near the base the apex rather suddenly ending in a rather long and slender point, which is also curved upwards; the upper cavity is deep and long; *H. philippinensis* Jac. is another closely allied species, which has the abdomen black, but the penis is of different shape, not having the apex produced into a curved and long point, but gradually tapering.

Haplosoma simplicipennis n. sp.

Entirely testaceous or flavous, head and thorax impunctate, elytra without longitudinal sulci, finely and rather closely punctured.

♂. The second abdominal segment with two short appendages.

Length 3-3 1/2 lines.

Head impunctate, frontal tubercles strongly raised, transverse, carina short, clypeus narrowly oblique, swollen, antennæ extending to the middle of the elytra, flavous, the third joint slightly shorter than the fourth, thorax of usual shape, the traverse sulcu-

tion deep, not quite extending to the margins, elytra rather strongly
and closely punctured, the apex not produced into a tooth, the
second abdominal segment furnished with two short, closely approached appendages, the first joint of the posterior tarsi as long as
the following two joints together, claws bifid.

Hab. Kanara, Belgaum, S. Bombay.

H. simplicipennis differs but little in shape and colour from
several other species of the genus, but can only be compared on
account of its uniform flavous coloration to *H. ceylonensis* Jac.,
H. longicornis All. and *H. rostripennis* All.; from the first named.
the species is distinguished by the want of the elytral costæ, from
the second by the much shorter antennæ; the want of the tooth
at the apex of the elytra, and the absence of the two longitudinal
sulci at the sides of the latter, separates the species from
H. rostripennis. The penis is very similar in shape to that of
H. abdominalis, but instead of being rather suddenly constricted
into a strongly curved point, is gradually narrowed and less
strongly curved; in the female the last abdominal segment is
deeply excavated at the apex and the latter is broadly rounded and
produced at the middle; numerous specimens were obtained, which
prove constant in the above particulars.

Haplosoma costatipennis n. sp.

Fulvous, abdomen black, elytra finely punctured, the sides with
a longitudinal costa, the apical angle dentiform.

Length 3 $1/2$-4 lines.

Head impunctate, the antennæ extending below the middle of the
elytra, the third and fourth joints equal, elongate, thorax one half
broader than long, of usual shape, the disc deeply transversely
sulcate, elytra rather opaque, finely punctured, the shoulders very
prominent, the sides with a very strongly marked longitudinal
costa, abbreviated before the apex, the latter slightly concave and
produced into a short tooth or point; abdomen black, the last
segment with a short indentation at the middle.

Hab. Madura (Madras).

This species may be compared to *H. ceylonensis* Jac. on account
of the elytral costæ, but in that insect the entire underside is
fulvous and the apical angle of the elytra is not produced; there are
only two (apparently female) specimens before me.

Mimastra alternata n. sp.

Testaceous, the antennæ and tarsi obscure piceous or fuscous,
thorax with five small piceous spots, elytra finely and closely

punctured, each with four double rows of longitudinal narrow fuscous stripes.

Length 4 lines.

Of elongate, parallel shape, the head impunctate, the vertex with a short central piceous spot, frontal tubercles trigonate, clypeus triangularly raised, antennæ slender, extending to the middle of the elytra, fuscous or piceous, the first joint long and slender, the second short, the third slightly shorter than the fourth joint, thorax subquadrate, one half broader than long, the lateral margin slightly rounded at the middle, the anterior angles obliquely produced, with a single seta, the surface not perceptibly punctured, with five small spots, of which two are placed close together before the middle, and the others transversely near the base, the outer spots being the largest, the central one the smallest of all, elytra very closely and finely punctured, the interstices very slightly longitudinally costate, with alternate longitudinal narrow double fuscous stripes, from base to apex, their epipleuræ very narrow, legs long and slender, finely pubescent, tibiæ unarmed, the first joint of the posterior tarsi as long as the following three joints together, claws appendiculate.

Hab. Madura, Madras Presidency.

This is an easily recognisable species on account of the striped elytra; there are ten specimens before me.

Cerophysa nigricornis n. sp.

Elongate, fulvous, the antennæ, tibiæ and tarsi black, thorax transversely bifoveolate, impunctate, elytra very finely punctured.

Length 2 1/2 lines.

Head impunctate, the frontal tubercles but little raised, clypeus triangularly swollen, sharply raised between the antennæ, palpi rather strongly incrassate, antennæ black, pubescent, not reaching to the middle of the elytra, the third and fourth joint equal, the eighth joint slightly longer than the others, terminal ones thickened, rather short; thorax about one half broader than long, the sides straight at the base, slightly rounded before the middle, the disc with a transverse short groove at each side, impunctate, reddish fulvous like the head, scutellum broad, elytra paler than the thorax, with a very slight metallic hue, finely punctured, legs black, the femora fulvous at the base, tibiæ unarmed, the metatarsus of the hind legs as long as the following joints together; anterior coxal cavities open.

Hab. Kanara, S. Bombay.

Of this species I have apparently only females before me and it is probable that the male has the eighth joint of the antennæ considerably enlarged as is usually the case in this genus, there is just a slight enlargement visible in the specimens before me; the species may be known by the reddish-fulvish head and thorax and the paler elytra.

Cerophysa nigricollis n. sp.

Black, the femora piceous, the abdomen flavous, thorax opaque, finely granulate, obsoletely sulcate, elytra metallic blue, closely punctured, the interstices slightly rugose.

Mas. The sixth and seventh joints of the antennæ dilated.

Length 2 lines.

♂. Head black, impunctate, shining, the frontal tubercles rather obsolete, transverse, clypeus with an acute central ridge, eyes large, antennæ scarcely extending to the middle of the elytra, black, the basal joint rather short, claviform, the second very short, the third elongate, the fourth shorter than the third, the fifth longer than the preceding joint and slightly dilated, the sixth longer than the seventh, both strongly widened (terminal joints wanting); thorax subquadrate, but little wider than long, the sides deflexed, the base slightly narrowed, the lateral margins nearly straight, the surface obsoletely depressed, black or nearly so, of a silky, opaque appearance, very minutely granulate and punctured, when seen under a strong lens, scutellum broad, black, elytra metallic blue, distinctly punctured in close and very irregular rows, the interstices slightly rugose, legs black, or piceous, the posterior femora and the abdomen flavous, the tibiæ unarmed, the first joint of the posterior tarsi longer than the following joints together.

Hab. Toungoo, Burmah.

In the female the antennæ have the sixth and seventh joints likewise dilated but to a much smaller degree and the legs and the abdomen are more or less black, but this latter colour may also occur probably in the male sex, in this the anterior tarsi have the first joint distinctly widened; the thorax in the present species has a peculiar silken appearance, caused by the fine granulate surface.

Astena(?) nigromaculata n. sp.

Fulvous, the antennæ (the basal joints excepted) and the abdomen black, head and thorax impunctate, elytra extremely finely and closely punctured, each with a broad longitudinal black band of variable width.

Var. The elytral band divided into two large spots.

Length 2-2 1/2 lines.

Head impunctate, the frontal tubercles distinct, but rather flat, transverse, clypeus triangular, palpi acute, the antennæ extending nearly to the end of the elytra, black, the lower three joints fulvous, the second and third one small, equal, the fourth as long as the preceding three joints together, pubescent like the following joints, thorax twice as broad as long, the sides and the posterior margin slightly rounded, the angles not prominent, the anterior ones very slightly thickened, the surface impunctate, fulvous, scutellum fulvous, elytra very finely and closely punctured, black, the margins very narrowly fulvous, their epipleuræ very broad and concave at the base, continued below the middle, the breast and the legs fulvous, the abdomen black, all the tibiæ mucronate, the first joint of the posterior tarsi longer than the following joints together, claws appendiculate, the last abdominal segment fulvous at the apex, the latter in the male incised at the sides, the middle lobe subquadrate.

Hab. Kanara, S. Bombay.

The black portion of the elytra seems subject to great variation, occupying in some specimens almost the entire disc and in others being divided or partly so, into two spots, an anterior small and a posterior larger one, or the band is greatly constricted at the middle although not divided. I have provisionally placed this species in *Aslena* with which it agrees in the main points, the second and third joint of the antennæ are however very short and equal, the elytral epipleuræ are very broad and the general shape of the insect is rather different, be this as it may, the species must at all events be placed amongst the *Luperinæ*.

Luperus Severini n. sp.

Testaceous, the antennæ (the basal joints excepted) black, thorax transverse, impunctate, elytra finely and very closely punctured, metatarsus of posterior legs very long.

Lenght 1 1/2 line.

Of posteriorly slightly widened shape, entirely flavous or testaceous, the head impunctate, the frontal elevations and the carina nearly contiguous, palpi piceous, antennæ black, the lower three joints and the base of the fourth, flavous, basal joint slender, second, slightly shorter than the third joint, fourth and fifth longer, equal, the following joints more slender, thorax twice as broad as long, the sides slightly rounded before the middle, nearly straight at the base, posterior angles acute, the surface with a few very minute punctures, very obsoletely depressed at each side, anteriorly, elytra very distinctly and closely punctured, legs slender; the posterior femora extending to the end of the abdomen, all the tibiæ mucronate, the first joint of the posterior tarsi, much longer than the following joints together, the anterior coxal cavities open.

Hab. Belgaum, S. Bombay.

A small species of somewhat the appearance of a *Monolepta* but possessing all the characters of *Luperus*; in the male, the thorax is only about half as broad as long; the metatarsus is longer than usual in this genus.

Luperus puncticollis n. sp.

Obscure piceous, the head, thorax and legs obscure testaceous, thorax transverse, closely punctured, elytra fuscous, closely and finely punctured.

Length 1 1/2 line.

Head impunctate, the frontal elevations very strongly raised, trigonate, clypeus swollen at its upper portion, antennæ extending to the middle of the elytra, fuscous, the lower two or three joints fulvous, basal joint long and slender, the second slightly thickened, but little shorter than the third joint, following joints nearly equal, thorax twice as broad as long, rather convex, the lateral margins moderately rounded, the angles not prominent, the surface proportionately strongly and rather closely punctured, fulvous, scutellum fulvous, rather broad, elytra darker than the thorax, obscure fuscous, more strongly and more closely punctured, rather convex, with a short depression below the scutellum, their epipleuræ continued below the middle, with a single row of punctures at the base, legs fulvous, all the tibiæ armed with a small spine, the first joint of the posterior tarsi as long as the following joints together, claws appendiculate.

Hab. Belgaum, S. Bombay.

A small species, of rather short and broad shape and principally distinguished by the strong punctuation of the thorax and elytra; I have not been able to discover any sexual characters, as those specimens I have examined were all females; the species resembles a good deal *L. pinicola* Duftsch. but is much more strongly punctured.

HEMYGASCELIS n. gen.

Elongate, subparallel, head prolonged, palpi filiform, antennæ as long as the body, slender, filiform, thorax one half longer than broad, subcylindrical, elytra irregularly punctured, their epipleuræ extremely narrow, legs long and slender, the tibiæ unarmed, the first joint of the posterior tarsi as long as the following two joints together, claws appendiculate, the anterior coxal cavities open.

Amongst the enormous number of Phytophaga, I know of no genus, *Megascelis* excepted, in which the head and thorax assumes such an elongate shape as in the case in the present genus, on account of which I cannot place the only species before me in *Phyllobotrica* with which it has all other characters in common; I would have however referred the present insect to *Konbirella* Duviv. likewise from India, had not the author described the tibiæ as mucronate (of wich I cannot discover a trace with the strongest lens) and the elytral epipleuræ as moderately broad, this portion being extremely narrow in the insect before me.

Hemygasoelis longicollis n. sp.

Fulvous, the antennæ, knees, tibiæ and tarsi black, head and thorax impunctate, elytra black, closely and finely punctured, the interstices slightly wrinkled.

♂. The metasternum produced into a triangular point, the abdomen deeply excavated, fringed with hairs.

Length 3 lines.

♂. Head not prolonged, of equal width, impunctate, the eyes rather small, frontal tubercles trigonate, distinct, clypeus triangularly widened, antennæ extending to the end of the elytra, black, the basal joint elongate, piceous, thickened at the apex, the second joint short, the third more than twice as long but slightly shorter than the fourth joint, following ones very elongate and slender; thorax one half longer than broad, subcylindrical, of equal width, the sides with an obsolete depression, the anterior and posterior angles thickened, the latter obsoletely rounded, the surface impunctate, fulvous, scutellum broad, fulvous, elytra wider at the base than the thorax, slightly dilated towards the apex, black, finely punctured and wrinkled throughout, underside and the anterior portion of the femora fulvous, abdomen deeply excavated, the sides of the excavation with long fringes of hairs, the base produced into an acute point, pygidium black.

Hab. Kanara, S. Bombay.

In the male, the head is contracted up to the eyes into the thorax, but if this is always the case, I am unable to say, the head in the female is very elongate, the tarsi are not widened and the metastermum as well as the abdomen is simple.

Haplosonyx indicus n. sp.

Entirely flavous, thorax very sparingly punctured, sulcate at the sides, elytra deeply and irregularly punctured at the base, punctate-striate posteriorly, the interstices partly transversely wrinkled and finely punctured.

Length 3-4 lines.

Head impunctate, with a deep fovea between the eyes, clypeus nearly impunctate, its anterior margin straight, antennæ not extending to the middle of the elytra, flavous, the second and third joints short, equal, the fourth the longest, terminal joints shortened; thorax more than twice as broad as long, the sides straight from the base to the middle, slightly rounded before the latter, the angles acute, the disc with a deep sulcation at the sides which does not extend to the middle and a small fovea in front of the scutellum, impressed with a few fine punctures only, scutellum triangular, impunctate, elytra with a very shallow and ill defined depression below the base, deeply and slightly geminate-punctate at the base, the rows becoming single below the middle but the punctures rather irregularly placed and often quite out of position, the punctuation close at the base, the interstices at the same place slightly transversely rugose and finely punctured at the lower portion; underside and legs flavous.

Hab. Belgaum, Southern Bombay.

H. indicus belongs to the smaller species of the genus and is closely allied to *H. varipes* Jac. and *H. inornatus* Jac. but differs from these and other species in the different sculpturing of the elytra which forms very closely approached double rows of deep punctures at the base, so that their geminate arrangement is somewhat difficult to see, the species differs further in the more rugose and finely punctured interstices from any of the other forms known, in connection with the comparative small size and uniform coloration. Three specimens were obtained.

KANARELLA n. gen.

Body elongate, antennæ filiform, long, the second and third joints small, equal, thorax subquadrate, narrowed at the base, the disc without depression, elytral epipleuræ continued below the middle, tibiæ unarmed, the metatarsus of the posterior legs longer than the following joints together, claws appendiculate, prosternum narrow, the anterior coxal cavities open.

This genus resembles somewhat the South American genus *Diabrotica* in general appearance and will enter Chapuis group the *Scelidina*; it has also most structural characters in common with the African genus *Megalognatha* but differs in the filiform antennæ and the long metatarsus of the posterior legs; the subquadrate posteriorly narrowed thorax is one of the characteristic points, peculiar to the genus.

Kanarella unicolor n. sp.

Testaceous, thorax subquadrate, impunctate, elytra broader than the thorax at the base, impunctate, antennæ nearly as long as the body.

Length 1 3/4-2 lines.

Head impunctate, the frontal tubercles rather broad, transverse, clypeus in shape of a triangular acutely raised ridge, antennæ extending below the middle of the elytra in the male, testaceous, the basal joint rather short and robust, the second and third very short, equal, the fourth joint as long as the preceding joints together and longer than the fifth joint, thorax scarcely broader than long, narrowed at the base, the lateral margins very slightly rounded before the middle, the anterior angles slightly oblique, not produced, anterior and posterior margins straight, the surface impunctate, scutellum broad, triangular, elytra much broader at the base than the thorax, slightly widened posteriorly, the shoulders rather prominent, the surface with some very minute and distantly placed punctures, only seen under a strong lens; the male organ long and slender, of equal width at the apex, the latter obliquely pointed.

Hab. Kanara, also Assam (my collection).

MADURASIA n. gen.

Shape and general appearance that of a small species of *Luperus*, antennæ filiform. all the joints with the exception of the first, of nearly equal length, thorax subquadrate, posterior angles obsolete, elytral epipleuræ very broad anteriorly, very narrow below the middle, posterior tibiæ with spine, the first joint of the posterior tarsi longer than the following joints, claws simple, anterior coxal cavities open.

Amongst the few genera of *Galerucinæ* having simple claws, the present one is closely allied to *Medythia* Jac. from Sumatra but differs in the shape of the thorax which is quite that of a species of *Luperus*, in *Medythia* this part is more elongate and strongly narrowed at the base, the general shape of the insect is also more convex and ovate and the elytral epipleuræ are differently constructed.

Madurasia obscurella n. sp.

Obscure testaceous, antennæ (the basal joints excepted) black, thorax extremely minutely punctured, elytra more distinctly but finely punctured with a very obscure longitudinal fuscous band near the suture.

Length 3/4-1 line.

Head impunctate at the vertex, the frontal tubercles distinct and rather elongate, lower portion of face finely pubescent, antennæ extending to the middle of the elytra, black or fuscous, the basal joints more or less testaceous, the second joint but slightly shorter than the third and following joints, the first joint the longest, thorax about one half broader than long, the sides nearly straight, the posterior margin rounded, anterior angles slightly obliquely thickened, furnished with a single seta, placed below the angle, posterior angles nearly obsolete, the surface very minutely punctured, testaceous, shining, the base with a small fovea near the posterior angles (sometimes absent), scutellum broader than long, elytra very finely and closely and more distinctly punctured than the thorax, the apex of each separately rounded, their epipleuræ broad at the base, indistinct below the middle, the surface very closely and finely punctured, pale testaceous, with an obscure, sometimes nearly obsolete, longitudinal fuscous band near the suture, which is slightly narrowed near the apical portion, legs long and slender, the posterior tibiæ mucronate, the metatarsus of the posterior legs longer than the following joints together, claws simple.

Hab. Madura, Madras Presidency.

CNEORIDES n. gen.

Body elongate, smooth, antennæ with the intermediate joints triangularly widened, thorax subquadrate, the sides subangulate before the middle, elytra closely punctured, with traces of pubescence, their epipleuræ continued to the apex, legs robust, the tibiæ mucronate, the metatarsus of the posterior legs not longer than the second joint, claws appendiculate, anterior coxal cavities open.

The general appearance of this insect, of which I possess a single apparently male specimen is somewhat that of a species of *Cneorane* but the antennæ are unlike any other of the numerous genera of *Galerucinæ* on account of the triangularly widened intermediate joints, this and the subquatrate non-impressed thorax, the mucronate tibiæ and structure of the tarsi, will assist in the recognition of the genus which would perhaps best find its place near *Nadrana* Baly.

Cneorides flaviventris n. sp.

Metallic dark blue, the abdomen flavous, thorax very finely
and subremotely punctured, elytra very closely and rather
strongly punctured.

Length 3 lines.

Head elongate, transversely grooved between the eyes, the
vertex impunctate, the frontal tubercles broad, not much raised,
nearly contiguous, clypeus broad, with a central ridge, its
anterior margin straight, labrum narrowly edged with fulvous,
penultimate joint of the palpi rather thick, terminal one short,
acute, antennæ closely approached at the base, inserted into deep
cavities and extending to the middle of the elytra, black, the
lower three joints stained with dark fulvous at the base and
apex, the basal joint short and thick, subcylindrical, the second
short, the third and fourth equal, elongate, the following five
joints shorter, triangularly widened, the terminal ones normal in
shape, thorax but little wider than long, the sides subangulate
before the middle, the posterior angles acute, slightly produced,
anterior and posterior margin nearly straight, the surface without
depression, finely and sparingly punctured, scutellum broader
than long, elytra much wider at the base than the thorax, very
closely, evenly and rather strongly punctured throughout, with
traces of longitudinal costæ at the posterior portion, their
epipleuræ broad, concave, and extending to the apex, underside
and legs metallic dark blue, abdomen flavous, the last segment
blackish, with a short median lobe, separated at the sides by a
deep groove.

Hab. Neelgherries,[India (my collection).

Liroëtes apicicornis n. sp.

Elongate, fulvous, shining; the last joint of the antennæ black,
thorax transverse, impunctate, elytra finely and rather closely
punctured.

Length 4 1/2 lines.

Head impunctate, the frontal tubercles broad, trigonate, strongly
raised, clypeus triangular, penultimate joint of the palpi strongly
incrassate, apical joint short, acute, antennæ extending to about
the middle of the elytra, fulvous, the first joint rather short and
thick, the second one half shorter than the third, fourth and
following joints equal, the last very elongate and black, pubescent, thorax more than twice as broad as long, the sides rounded,
the anterior angles thickened and produced into a short tooth,
the anterior margin slightly concave or sinuate at the middle,

the surface rather convex, impunctate, scutellum broad, elytra wider at the base than the thorax, convex, closely and finely but distinctly punctured, underside and legs fulvous, tibiæ unarmed, the first joint of the posterior tarsi, longer than the following joints together, claws appendiculate, the anterior coxal cavities open.

Hab. Kanara, S. Bombay.

Closely allied to *L. fulvipennis* Jac. from China, of the same shape and colour, but the antennæ fulvous as well as the legs, the apical joint of the former black only, the thorax more transverse and shorter.

Galeruca himalayensis n. sp.

Black, apterous, thorax much narrowed at the base, rugose-punctate, the middle smooth, deeply depressed in the female, elytra without costæ, closely rugose, the interstices raised in short striæ.

Length 3-4 lines.

♂. Head strongly rugose, the vertex with a deep, smooth triangular depression at the middle, frontal elevations strongly raised, smooth, fulvous, antennæ robust, the third and fourth joints, equal, the second one half shorter, the terminal four joints wanting, thorax rather more than twice as broad as long, the sides much narrowed at the base, rounded and produced before the middle, the posterior margin strongly concave in front of the scutellum; the disc with a deep lateral fovea and a small depression at the middle, the latter nearly impunctate, the sides strongly rugosely punctate, scutellum twice as broad as long, elytra rather flattened, widened posteriorly, with a narrow, raised margin extending to the base and to the scutellum, the whole surface closely rugosely punctured, with rows of short, longitudinal striæ, irregularly placed, the interspaces also transversely wrinkled or rugose, intermediate tibiæ with a spine, the others unarmed, the first joint of the posterior tarsi as long as the following two joints together, claws bifid, anterior coxal cavities closed.

Hab. Dalhousie, Himalayas.

This species seems allied to *G. monticola* Kiesenw. which is like-wise apterous and agrees with it in several other details ; but has pubescent antennæ and a differently sculptured head and thorax, I am however not acquainted with the species which is not likely to be identical with the present insect, since *G. monticola* inhabits the Pyrenaees; there is a good deal of difference to be seen in the sculpturing of the thorax between the two sexes, the female having the disc almost entirely and deeply depressed by a smooth sulcation, impressed with a few punctures; there are however only two specimens before me, and I am unable to say, whether this is always the case.

Aenidea violaceipennis n. sp.

Fulvous or flavous, thorax impunctate, deeply foveolate, elytra with basal depression, violaceous-blue, extremely minutely and subremotely punctured.

♂. Head deeply excavated in front, palpi strongly widened, antennæ with the intermediate joints curved.

Length 2 1/2-3 lines.

Head impunctate, the entire lower portion deeply excavate, the interior of the excavation furnished with two upper and two lower laminæ or flattened plates, penultimate joint of the palpi enormously dilated, the antennæ fulvous, nearly as long as the entire body, the basal joint long, gradually thickened, the second extremely short; the following joints all slightly curved, the terminal ones thinner, thorax one half broader than long, the sides slightly narrowed at the base, but little rounded in front, the surface deeply transversely sulcate, impunctate, flavous, the sulcation not extending to the sides, scutellum triangular, flavous, elytra with a rather deep depression below the base, dark violaceous-blue, the surface very finely granulate and minutely punctured, when seen under a strong lens, underside and legs fulvous, the first joint of the posterior tarsi much longer than the following joints, anterior coxal cavities closed.

Hab. Toungoo.

This species is closely allied to *A. barbata* Baly from Assam but differs in not having the intraocular space swollen, as in that species, the head is also differently structured in regard to the excavation, as well as the antennæ, and the elytra are of different colour. The female is unknown to me.

Aenidea truncatipennis n. sp.

Elongate, parallel, fulvous, the antennæ, the apex of the tibiæ and the tarsi black, thorax obsoletely biimpressed, elytra metallic blue or green, finely and closely punctured, abdomen bluish black.

Var. Above and below pale fulvous, with a slight metallic hue, antennæ more or less fulvous.

♂. Head deeply excavated, the clypeus extending inwards in shape of a short projection fringed with hairs, the interior of the cavity with two elongate processes.

Length 2 1/2-3 lines.

Head of the male broad, fulvous, the vertex impunctate, not
constricted, the lower portion deeply excavated through its entire
width, from the base of wich two lanzeolate projections, fringed
with hairs are visible, they lay however flat upon the floor of the
cavity and are rather difficult to see, at the sides a short continua-
tion of the clypeus extends inwards at right angle the edges of
which are fringed with long hairs, palpi swollen, antennæ nearly
extending to the apex of the elytra, black, the basal joint
long and curved, the second short, the third and following
joints elongate, slightly widened anteriorly, pubescent, thorax
scarcely longer than broad, distinctly narrowed at the base, the
sides straight at the latter place, rounded before the middle, the
surface obsoletely biimpressed at the sides, fulvous, minutely
granulate and impunctate, the lateral margins with some short
hairs, scutellum broad, elytra very closely and finely punctured,
the punctuation somewhat regularly arranged in rows near the
suture, their apex separately truncately rounded not covering the
pygidium, tibiæ unarmed, the first joint of the posterior tarsi as
long as the following joints together, anterior cavities closed.

Hab. Kanara, Belgaum, S. Bombay.

The structure of the head in the male differs from several other
species which have a similar excavation and of which several
are now known all showing this extraordinary and varying
structural peculiarity; the female specimens before me have a
simple head, the antennæ are shorter and the general size is
larger, but no other differences are noticeable; the colour is
however subject to much variation, as some specimens are entirely
fulvous without scarcely a trace of the metallic tint of the elytra
and of the abdomen.

Aenidea pilicornis n. sp.

Elongate, obscure fulvous, antennæ longer than the body, the
apical joints darker, thorax transverse, bifoveolate, impunctate,
elytra extremely finely punctured.

♂. Head deeply excavated at its lower portion, the middle of
the cavity divided into an anterior and posterior half, basal joint
of the antennæ with a fringe of long hairs.

Length 2 3/4 lines.

Head very broad, impunctate, the frontal tubercles strongly
raised, transverse, eyes large, lower portion of the face deeply
excavated through its entire width, the upper half divided from the
lower by a semicircularly emarginate edge, exposing another
cavity within, palpi incrassate at the penultimate joint, antennæ

extending beyond the elytra, the basal joint rather short and thick, furnished at its lower margin with a fringe of stiff long hairs, second joint short, provided as well as the following joints with two very long bristles, intermediate joints very elongate, truncate at the apex, terminal joints thin, the last four blackish, thorax nearly twice as broad as long, the sides narrowed at the base, rounded anteriorly, the surface impunctate, bifoveolate at the sides, scutellum broadly triangulate, elytra very finely and closely punctured, the apex subtruncate, with a few stiff hairs as well as the lateral margin, their epipleuræ very broad, continued to the apex, legs pubescent, tibiæ unarmed, the first joint of the posterior tarsi as long as the following three joints together, anterior coxal cavities closed.

Hab. Bombay (my collection).

Only a single male specimen of this species is known to me.

Aenidea pallida n. sp.

Testaceous, thorax obsoletely bifoveolate, impunctate, elytra very minutely punctured.

♂. Head deeply excavated anteriorly, the bottom of the excavation with a longitudinal ridge, basal joint of the antennæ piceous, fringed with hairs.

Length 3 lines.

Of pale testaceous colour; the head impunctate, the frontal elevations narrowly transverse, the lower portion of the face in the male deeply excavated, the inner portion bounded by a semicircular ridge above, the clypeus extending inwards in a slightly raised central ridge, apex of the mandibles black, palpi moderately swollen at the penultimate joint, antennæ testaceous, extending to the middle of the elytra, the first joint rather short and thick, piceous, with a fringe of hairs at the lower margin, second joints hort, third slightly longer than the fourth joint, the following ones cylindrical, of equal length; thorax one half broader than long, distinctly narrowed at the base, the disc with two nearly contiguous shallow foveæ, impunctate, minutely granulate, scutellum triangular, elytra very finely and closely punctured, their epipleuræ very broad, continued to the apex, the first joint of the posterior tarsi as long as the following three joints.

Hab. Belgaum, S. Bombay.

Very closely allied to *A. pilicornis* but of more elongate shape and of very pale colour, the antennæ without the long bristles and of different comparative length in regard to the joints, but the excavated portion of the head almost similar; the female has as usual a simple head, the clypeus is comparatively broad and the antennæ are without the fringe of hairs at the base.

I should have considered this species identical with *A. pilicornis* had not the antennæ shown the above mentioned differences, the joints in the allied species are also rather suddenly thickened at the apex which is not the case in the present insect.

Aenidea rufofulva n. sp.

Fulvous, thorax bifoveolate, impunctate, elytra extremely finely punctured, clypeus of the male strongly raised into a triangular transverse projection.

Length 3 lines.

Head impunctate, frontal elevations transverse, distinctly raised, clypeus strongly raised, forming a horizontal pointed ridge, palpi strongly swollen, antennæ extending to two thirds the length of the elytra, rather thin and slender, the second joint short, the third and fourth equal, following joints but slightly shorter, thorax one half broader than long, narrowed at the base, the surface impunctate, rather deeply bifoveolate, elytra closely and finely punctured, the first joint of the posterior tarsi as long as the following joints together, tibiæ unarmed, anterior coxal cavities closed.

Hab. Belgaum, S. Bombay.

Of dark fulvous colour and of the same shape and sculpture as the preceding two species, but at once distinguished by the structure of the clypeus in the male; the female has a simple clypeus but does not differ otherwise.

Aenidea dilaticornis n. sp.

Pale testaceous, thorax subquadrate, bifoveolate, impunctate, elytra minutely punctured.

♂. Head deeply excavated anteriorly, antennæ with the intermediate joints moderately widened, the apical ones slender.

Length 2 1/2 lines.

Smaller than *A. pallida* but of similar shape and colour, the head impunctate, the frontal tubercles narrowly transverse, the eyes large, fulvous, the lower portion of the face deeply excavated, the antennæ extending beyond the end of the elytra, flavous, the first joint rather long, club-shaped, the second very short, the third and fourth elongate, equal, fifth, shorter, all the joints rather flattened, the apex of each truncate, the terminal two joints much thinner and more slender, thorax one half broader than long, narrowed at the base, the disc deeply bifoveolate, impunctate, elytra very finely and closely punctured.

Hab. Belgaum, S. Bombay.

This species can only be separated from *A. pallida* by its smaller size and the different structure of the antennæ, all the joints of the latter are, with the exception of the last two, robust and somewhat widened while the terminal ones are slender and tapering; in *A. pallida* the joints are cylindrical, also much less elongate and shorter.

Aenidea modesta n. sp.

Pale testaceous or flavous, thorax transversely biimpressed, impunctate, elytra finely and closely punctured.

♂. Head simple, the antennæ as long as the elytra, robust at the intermediate joints.

Length 2 lines.

Again of similar colour and shape than the preceding species, but the head not excavated, the space between the antennæ raised, the clypeus deflexed, the eyes very large, palpi robust, antennæ extending to the apex of the elytra, very robust, the first joint short and thick, the second extremely short, moniliform, third and following joints robust, the apical ones slender. more elongate, thorax one half broader than long, of similar shape as the preceding species, the discoidal depressions rather deeper and transversely shaped, elytra closely and finely punctured, the last abdominal segment of the male with a short oblique incision at the sides, the median lobe subquadrate, flat.

Hab. Belgaum, S. Bombay.

I am obliged to separate this species again from any of the preceding on account of the simple head of the male; the antennæ agree nearly with that of *A. dilaticornis* but the joints are shorter, especially the basal joint which in the last named species is much more slender and club-shaped, the second joint in the present insect is also extremely short, and the impression of the thorax is more of the shape of a transverse short sulcus; as females, belonging to this species, I refer several specimens which agree in the sculpture of the thorax, and have much shorter and thinner antennæ.

Acroxena indica n. sp.

Fulvous, thorax obsoletely foveolate, impunctate, elytra very minutely punctured.

Mas. Face below the antennæ, with an acute hornlike projection, clypeus swollen, its anterior edge raised into a point at the middle, third joint of the antennæ emarginate.

Length 4 lines.

Head impunctate, the frontal tubercles distinct, trigonate, lower portion of the face concave, with a short, lanceolate appendage of elongate shape, clypeus separated from the face by a semicircular deep groove, swollen and raised at the middle into a point, labrum scarcely visible, black, as well as the apex of the mandibles, penultimate joint of the palpi, incrassate, antennæ long, nearly extending to the end of the elytra, fulvous, the basal joint long and curved, the second very short, the third as long or rather longer than the first joint, emarginate near the apex, the following joints shorter, thorax one half broader than long, narrowed at the base, the sides straight at the same place, rounded before the middle, the angles tuberculiform, with a single seta, the surface with two obsolete depressions at the middle, impunctate, scutellum broad, triangular, elytra very minutely and rather closely punctured, tibiæ unarmed, the first joint of the posterior tarsi as long as the following two joints together, claws appendiculate, the metasternum smooth and shining, furnished with two short, horn-like appendages at the middle, anterior coxal cavities closed.

Hab. Kanara.

Of this interesting species, only males are contained in this collection; the insect is allied to *A. nasuta* Baly but differs in the structure of the head, and in the finely punctured elytra, the lower joints of the antennæ are in some specimens stained with piceous below; I scarcely think this genus can be separated from *Aenidea* or *Platyxantha* since the differences are only sexual and peculiar to the male insect, these vary in almost every species, all other generic structures are identical; Baly says that the shape of *Acroxena* is distinct from *Aenidea*, being more elongate, but this character in itself is of no value, since shape is as variable as colour in the Phytophaga.

Candezea multipunctata n. sp.

Fulvous, the elytra, breast and abdomen black, thorax finely punctured, obsoletely depressed at the sides, elytra closely and strongly punctured, the interstices minutely punctate.

Var. Abdomen more or less flavous at the sides.

Length 2 lines.

Head impunctate, fulvous, the frontal elevations narrowly transverse, clypeus distinctly raised between the antennæ, labrum more or less piceous, antennæ fuscous, the lower three or four joints flavous, basal joint slender, second joint short, third, one half longer, fourth and following joints longer than the two preceding joints together, finely pubescent, thorax scarcely twice as broad as long, the sides straight, the posterior margin strongly rounded, anterior angles oblique, slightly thickened, the surface with a very obsolete transverse depression at the sides, very finely and obsoletely punctured, flavous or fulvous, scutellum flavous, elytra elongate, convex, closely and comparatively strongly punctured, the interstices also very finely punctured, black, their epipleuræ continued below the middle, legs long and slender, fulvous, the metatarsus of the posterior legs long, all the tibiæ mucronate.

Hab. Belgaum, S. Bombay.

This species may be known from other similarly coloured allied forms, by the sculpturing of the elytra.

Candezea fuscipennis n. sp.

Elongate, testaceous, thorax transverse, very sparingly punctured, elytra obscure brownish or fuscous, very finely and subremotely punctured, the apex of each pointed.

Length 1 1/2 line.

Head impunctate, the frontal tubercles small, transverse, the clypeus with a rather long and acute central ridge, antennæ extending beyond the middle of the elytra, testaceous, the apex of the terminal joint piceous, basal joint slender, the second short, the third scarcely one half longer, the fourth and following joints elongate, thorax at least twice as broad as long, the lateral margins nearly straight, the posterior one slightly rounded, the anterior angles obliquely truncate, slightly thickened, the disc with some very shallow depressions at the sides, more or less distinct, impunctate, testaceous, scutellum broader than long, elytra obscure fuscous, finely but not very closely punctured, the apex of each pointed (in most specimens), their epipleuræ very broad and concave, continued below the middle, legs long and slender, all the tibiæ mucronate, the first joint of the posterior tarsi longer than the following joints together, claws appendiculate, the anterior coxal cavities closed.

Hab. Belgaum, Kanara, S. Bombay.

The general appearance of this species is rather delicate and suggestive of a *Luperus*, the thorax is more transverse than is usual the case in *Candezea* and shows in some specimens a slight transverse depression, the colour is testaceous but that of the elytra is fuscous or brownish, the species possesses all the structural characters of *Candezea*.

Candezea pilosa n. sp.

Testaceous, pubescent, thorax deeply bifoveolate, elytra pubescent, narrowly margined with black, breast black at the sides, or testaceous.

♂. Anterior tarsi dilated at the first joint.

Length 2 lines.

♂. Head impunctate, opaque, the frontal elevations distinct, trigonate, clypeus depressed, broad, with a more or less distinct central ridge, labrum piceous, eyes very large, the intermediate space narrower than their diameter, antennæ slender, the first and second joint small, equal, testaceous, the following six joints piceous, the rest broken off, thorax twice as broad as long, the sides nearly straight, slightly narrowed near the anterior angles, the latter thickened, with a single seta, basal margin rounded, the disc with a deep fovea at each side, the surface not perceptibly punctured, opaque, scutellum black, elytra closely covered with yellowish pubescence, the basal margin, a spot on the shoulders and the sutural and lateral margins narrowly black, epipleuræ also margined with black, continued to the apex, legs and underside testaceous, the breast black at the sides, the first joint of the anterior tarsi much widened, the metatarsus of the posterior legs, longer than half the tibiæ.

Hab. Belgaum.

The species, described here, is evidently closely allied to several other pubescent forms from New Guinea, described by me in Zoolog. Novitat., Vol. I. It differs however in the impunctate thorax, its deeply foveolate sides, the short second and third joints of the antennæ, the want of elytral markings etc. and in the dilated anterior tarsi of the male; in the specimen, which seems to belong to the other sex, the antennæ, elytra and the underside are nearly entirely testaceous, the elytra show however just traces of the dark margins; the thorax instead of two deep foveæ, has a short transverse sulcation, not divided, in other respects there are no differences, those present, are no doubt sexual.

Monolepta fulvifrons n. sp.

Black, the head fulvous, thorax finely punctured, obsoletely transversely depressed, elytra very closely and distinctly punctured.

Length 2 lines.

Moderately convex, entirely black, with the exception of the head which is reddish-fulvous, the vertex finely punctured, frontal elevations strongly transverse, very narrow, bounded by a deep groove behind, clypeus in shape of a strongly raised triangular ridge, labrum black, antennæ extending tho the middle of the clytra, black, the basal joint rather elongate, the second, one half shorter than the third one, fourth and following joints distinctly longer than the third, thorax twice as broad as long, the sides slightly rounded, the angles thickened, the disc with an obsolete transverse depression at the middle of each side, finely, rather obsoletely and closely punctured, scutellum broad, impunctate, elytra very closely and more distinctly punctured than the thorax, their epipleuræ indistinct below the midde, underside and legs black, the first joint of the posterior tarsi much longer than the following joints together.

Hab. N. W. Provinces.

The entirely black colour and the reddish head will distinguish this species from any of its allies.

Monolepta picturata n. sp.

Rufous, the antennæ (the basal joints excepted), the tibiæ and tarsi and the breast, black, head and thorax rufous, elytra black, each clytron with two spots at the base, one at the sides and a subsutural, posteriorly widened stripe near the apex, yellowish-white.

Length 1 1/2 line.

Head impunctate, rufous, frontal tubercles narrowly transverse, clypeus with a distinct central ridge, labrum black, antennæ extending to the middle of the elytra, black, the lower three joints flavous, the third joint twice as long as the second one, fourth joint double the length of the preceding one, the following nearly equally elongate, thorax twice as broad as long, of equal width, the sides straight, the anterior angles oblique, the surface extremely finely and closely punctured, rufous, scutellum black, elytra very finely and closely punctured, black, two spots at the base, one at the side sand a narrow stripe placed near the suture at the posterior portion and being suddenly widened at the apex, yellowish, of the spots, one of rather elongate shape is placed on the shoulder, another larger one, longer than broad, near the scutellum, the spot at the side is slightly transverse and situated immediately below the middle near the lateral margin, the subsutural band begins at the middle but does not touch the suture nor the apex with its widened end, the breast black as well as the tibiæ and tarsi, the former however are flavous at the base, the metatarsus of the posterior legs very elongate, elytra epipleuræ indistinct below the middle, anterior coxal cavities closed.

Hab. Toungoo.

A plainly marked species, resembling somewhat in coloration *M. signata* Oliv. but easily distinguished by the number, position and shape of the elytral pale spots.

Monolepta kanarensis n. sp.

Broadly ovate, convex, entirely dark fulvous, the antennæ (the first joint excepted) black, thorax impunctate, elytra very finely and closely punctured.

Length 2 lines.

Head impunctate, the frontal elevations feebly raised, eyes very large, antennæ closely approached at the base, extending below the middle of the elytra, black, the basal joint fulvous, the second and third extremely small, equal, the fourth, as long as the preceding joints together, pubescent, the following nearly as elongate, thorax about one half broader than long, rather convex, the lateral margin nearly straight, the posterior one rounded, the anterior angles slightly oblique, the surface impunctate, shining, elytra somewhat strongly convex, very minutely and closely punctured, their epipleuræ indistinct below the middle, legs slender, fulvous, the tibiæ and tarsi slightly darker, the first joint of the posterior tarsi extremely long; penis long and slender, the apex obliquely pointed.

Hab. Kanara, S. Bombay.

This *Monolepta* seems closely allied to *M. castanea* Alld. from Singapoor, but differs in the fulvous underside and legs and in the shining and impunctate thorax, the posterior angles of the latter are distinct, otherwise the species might as well been placed in *Ochralea*.

Monolepta Andrewesi n. sp.

Flavous or fulvous, thorax extremely finely punctured, obsoletely depressed, elytra black, very closely and finely punctured, breast and sometimes the abdomen partly black.

Length 1 ⅟₂-2 lines.

Head impunctate, the frontal tubercles small but distinct, carina short and rather broad, antennæ extending to about two-thirds the length of the elytra, fulvous, the second and third joint short, the fourth as long as slightly longer than the preceding two joints, the following joints elongate and slender, thorax twice as broad as long, the sides slightly, the posterior margin more strongly rounded, the surface with an obsolete transverse depression at the middle, very finely and closely punctured, scutellum black, elytra convex, rather more distinctly punctured than the thorax and as closely so, black, shining, their epipleuræ indistinct below the middle, legs fulvous, the metatarsus of the posterior ones long, the breast and the abdomen at the middle, black.

Hab. Kanara, S. Bombay.

This *Monolepta* resembles in coloration very nearly several other Eastern forms, especially *Candezea nigripennis* Jac. from New Guinea, but the elytral epipleuræ in that species are continued below the middle and the thorax is impunctate; the present species in moreover distinguished by the black elytra and the similarly coloured breast, this colour also extending to a greater or smaller degree to the abdominal segments; a good many specimens were obtained.

Monolepta maculosa Allard.

A most variable species in regard to colour; the following are the varieties before me.

Testaceous, the base of the elytra with a dark brown subquadrate spot (typical form).

Elytra with another spot near the apex.

Elytra with all the margins narrowly piceous.

Elytra entirely testaceous.

Allard has described his type from the same locality, Belgaum, where M. Andrewes specimens were obtained, others are before me from Kanara. To the description of the author I may add, that the antennæ have the second and third joints rather short, the latter is however slightly longer in the female than in the male, the thorax shows a more or less distinct transverse depression at each side and is twice as broad as long with the sides nearly straight, the male organ is long and slender and gradually narrowed at the apex, the latter of which is truncate, the underside likewise varies from pale to nearly black; the variety in which the elytra are without spots but have a narrow piceous sutural and lateral margin, looks at first sight as a totally different species, but some intermediate forms before me and the examination of the penis prooves the identity of both forms.

Monolopta orientalis Jac. var. *konbirensis* Duviv.

Several specimens which I received from M. Duvivier as varieties of his *M. konbirensis* are identical with my *M. orientalis* described in 1889, but the typical form of Duvivier's species is entirely without the elytral transverse flavous band and looks at first sight like another species and although the author says that his species is extremely variable he does not mention the variety with a flavous band of which he has send me specimens under the name of *konbirensis*; in a latter paper on Indian species by Duvivier, he also separates the two species, but except the difference of coloration mentioned above I can seen no other distinctions in regard to structure, etc. M. Andrewes specimens were obtained at Belgaum.

Monolepta piceo-maculata n. sp.

Testaceous, the antennæ (the basal joints excepted) the tibiæ and tarsi more or less black, thorax finely punctured, the sides black, elytra finely and closely punctured, a spot at the middle of the base, another at the middle of the disc, the apex and the lateral margins anteriorly, piceous.

Length 1 1/2 line.

Head impunctate; testaceous, the vertex with a piceous spot, eyes very large, the space dividing them, narrower than their diameter, frontal tubercles trigonate, distinct, labrum piceous, antennæ closely approached at the base, extending to the middle of the elytra, blackish, the lower three joints testaceous, basal joint long and slender, second and third, small, equal, the former thickened; thorax twice as broad as long, the lateral margins rounded, with a narrow black band, anterior angles thickened, oblique, posterior ones acute, the surface finely punctured and slightly rugose, scutellum black, elytra sculptured in the same way as the thorax, the extreme sutural and basal margin, a spot placed at the middle of the latter, another on the shoulder and a third larger one at the middle, nearly joined to a smaller spot a little lower near the sides, piceous, the apex and the lateral margin at the base, of the same colour, epipleuræ indistinct below the middle, legs and abdomen testaceous, the breast more or less piceous, the metatarsus of the posterior legs long.

Hab. Belgaum, S. Bombay.

Closely allied to *M. timorensis* Jac. (Novit. Zoolog., Vol. I) but the sides of the thorax black, and the elytral markings of different shape, not forming bands, although placed similarly; the five specimens before me show no differences in this respect.

Monolepta trifasciata n. sp.

Head and the breast black, the thorax, legs and abdomen flavous, elytra extremely closely and finely punctured, yellowish-white, a transverse band at the base, another at the middle, the apex and the margins, piceous.

Var. Elytra black, each with two pale yellow spots.

Length 1 1/4 line.

Head impunctate, black, the frontal tubercles rather broad and flat, bounded by a transverse shallow groove behind, clypeus extending into a distinctly raised ridge between the antennæ, labrum and palpi black, antennæ extending rather below the middle of the elytra, black, the lower four joints flavous, basal joint long, second and third joint short and equal, fourth as long as the preceding two joints together, thorax transverse, twice as broad as long, the sides very slightly rounded, the angles rather obtuse, the surface finely and closely punctured, with an obsolete shallow depression at each side, scutellum black, shining, elytra parallel, extremely closely and finely punctured, flavous, with three transverse dark bands, the first at the base, widened towards the suture, the second one at the middle, narrow and of equal width and the third at the extreme apex, these bands extend to the sides and are connected with the similarly coloured lateral margin; the pygidium is likewise black, the femora and the abdomen flavous, tibiæ and tarsi fuscous, the metatarsus of the posterior legs longer than the following joints, elytral epipleuræ indistinct below the middle.

Hab. Belgaum, S. Bombay.

This species has the elytral bands more or less connected, so that in the variety there are two pale yellow round spots, at the middle and near the apex, placed on a black ground colour, but when the pale colour predominates, the black portion consists of three narrow transverse black bands; it may be that this form is the real variety and the other, the normal one.

Monolepta indica n. sp.

Testaceous or pale flavous, the base of the head, the terminal joints of the antennæ and the breast black, thorax extremely minutely punctured, elytra very closely and finely punctate, the margins narrowly obscure piceous.

Length 1 1/2 line.

Narrowly elongate and parallel, the head impunctate, black at the vertex, the frontal tubercles, strongly raised as well as the clypeus, the latter and the labrum piceous, antennæ extending beyond the middle of the elytra, black, the lower four joints flavous, second and third joint small, fourth and following joints elongate, pubescent, thorax twice as broad as long, the sides and the posterior margin slightly rounded, the surface extremely finely punctured, with a scarcely perceptible depression at each side, scutellum black, elytra very closely and more distinctly punctured than the thorax, all the margins narrowly piceous, their epipleuræ broad anteriorly, indistinct below the middle, legs pale fulvous, abdomen testaceous, breast black, the metatarsus of the posterior legs very long; the male organ convex at the middle, long and slender anteriorly, the apex suddenly constricted and again widened into a narrow spoon-shaped point.

Hab. Kanara, Belgaum, S. Bombay.

M. indica is closely allied in coloration to *M. melanocephala* Jac. from Sumatra, but that species is of rather larger size, the thorax has a very distinct lateral depression and the tibiæ and tarsi are black.

Monolepta longitarsis n. sp.

Ovate, very convex, chestnut-brown, thorax impunctate, the sides straight, elytra very finely and closely punctured, their epipleuræ absent below the middle, metatarsus of the posterior legs extremely long.

Length 1 1/2 line.

Head impunctate, the eyes very large, closely approached, the clypeus broad and extending upwards between the antennæ; the latter closely approached, long and slender, the basal joint very long the second and third joints rather short, equal, the fourth as long as the preceding two joints together, thorax twice as broad as long, the lateral margins straigt, distinctly narrowed in front, the anterior margin about one half shorter than the posterior one, the latter rounded and produced at the middle, the surface impunctate, scutellum elongate, triangular, elytra very convex, subcylindrical, chestnut-brown, finely and closely punctured, their epipleuræ broad at the base but disappearing below the middle, legs long and slender, the tibiæ mucronate, the spine at the posterior tibiæ very long, the first joint of the posterior tarsi nearly as long as the tibia; the penis subcylindrical, moderately long, not widened at the apex, the latter very little pointed, rather broad and forming a short angle at the sides.

Hab. Belgaum, S. Bombay.

I have no doubt, that some authors would have placed this species in a new genus on account of the structure of the head and the very long metatarsus, but I for my part see no reason to remove the species from *Monolepta* as the above differences are only those of degrees which in the exotic species may be multiplied into new genera at nearly every species.

Hymenesia limbata n. sp.

Fulvous, the antennæ, apex of the femora and the tibiæ and tarsi black, thorax closely punctured, with two obscure bluish spots, elytra finely pubescent, and rugose, violaceous black, narrowly margined with fulvous.

Length 4 lines.

Of elongate, parallel shape, the head rather strongly and closely punctured at the middle, pale fulvous, frontal elevations broad, trigonate, divided by a central narrow groove, which extends upwards to the vertex, clypeus transverse, strongly raised, antennæ extending to two-thirds the length of the elytra, black, the basal joint short and thick, the second less than half the size, third joint one half shorter than the fourth, this the longest and like the following four joints widened and flattened, three terminal joints much shorter and also widened and flat, thorax three times broader than long, the sides nearly straight, the anterior margin deeply concave, posterior one parallel to it, the surface obsoletely depressed at the middle and at the sides, very closely and finely punctured, the depressions at the sides, marked with a small obscure bluish spot, anterior angles tuberculiform, scutellum flavous, broad, pubescent, its apex broadly rounded, elytra very finely rugose, clothed with fine and short yellow pubescence, violaceous, black, all the margins narrowly flavous, underside and legs pale fulvous, finely pubescent, the posterior portion of the femora and the tibiæ and tarsi black, tibiæ unarmed, the first joint of the posterior tarsi as long as the following two joints together, claws bifid, anterior coxal cavities open.

Hab. Panugdé, Burmah.

A single male specimen was obtained by M. Andrewes; it agrees in all essential characters with the only other species (*H. tranquebarica* Fab.) of this genus, but the antennæ are of rather different structure, the ninth joint is not as short as the second as in the type, but is as large as the following apical joints and equally widened and flattened, although much shorter than the preceding joints; I did not think it wise to establish another genus on this difference alone; the male has the last abdominal segment deeply excavated, the protruding apex of the penis is flattened and obliquely pointed.

Hyphænia obscuripennis n. sp.

Fuscous-violaceous, the head, basal joints of the antennæ, thorax and the legs flavous, thorax transversely sulcate, impunctate, elytra obscure fuscous, finely and subremotely punctured.

Length 1 1/2 line.

Head flavous, impunctate, frontal elevations narrowly transverse, clypeus triangular, narrow, antennæ not quite extending

to the apex of the elytra, finely pubescent, fuscous, the lower three
joints flavous, the basal joint rather short, club-shaped, second
joint very short, third joint nearly as long as the fourth, elongate
like the rest of the joints, thorax subquadrate, one half broader
than long, the sides slightly concave at the base, very little rounded
anteriorly, the disc transversely depressed, shining, impunctate,
elytra fuscous, with a violaceous gloss, finely but not very closely
punctured, legs slender, the femora flavous, tibiæ and tarsi fuscous,
the tibiæ unarmed, the metatarsus of the posterior legs as long as
the following two joints together, claws appendiculate, anterior
coxal cavities closed, underside obscure fulvous, the last abdominal
segment with a longitudinal depression.

Hab. Belgaum.

Although the antennæ in this species are not covered with such
long fringes of hairs as in the typical form, they are nevertheless
pubescent, and the structural characters of *Hyphænia* are all
present; the two specimens obtained, make the impression of being
immature, on account of the uncertain colour of the elytra, but as
both are exactly similar in this respect, it is no doubt the normal
colour of the species, the latter is much smaller than *H. submetal-
lica* Jac. from Burmah, the antennæ are shorter and less pubescent,
the thorax has not two foveæ but is transversely sulcate, besides
other differences which are present.

Cneorane varipes n. sp.

Metallic blue, the antennæ (the basal joints excepted) the four
anterior tibiæ and the posterior legs, black, head and thorax fulvous, elytra metallic dark blue, irregularly and closely punctured.

Length 3 lines.

Of parallel shape, the head impunctate, fulvous, the frontal
tubercles narrowly oblique, strongly raised, clypeus with an acute
central ridge, antennæ extending below the middle of the elytra,
black, the lower three joints fulvous below, the third joint shorter
than the fourth one, thorax about one half broader than long, the
sides but slightly rounded at the middle, the anterior margin
straight, the anterior angles slightly tuberculiform, the surface
entirely impunctate, shining, scutellum piceous, broad, its apex
rounded, elytra not depressed below the base, shining, dark blue,
distinctly and rather closely punctured, the punctures somewhat
arranged in rows near the suture, but irregularly at the rest of the
surface, the interstices here and there wrinkled, the four anterior
femora fulvous, the outer margin of their tibiæ and the tarsi blackish,
the posterior legs entirely bluish black, the breast and abdomen
metallic blue, finely punctured.

Hab. N. West. Provinces.

There are now a considerable number of species known, belonging to this genus, all being nearly identical in coloration, so that it becomes more and more difficult to separate them, the present one resembles greatly *C. femoralis* Jac. in its system of coloration but is much smaller and of nearly parallel shape, the thorax has the sides much less rounded and produced, the elytra are not depressed below the base and of dark blue, not violaceous colour and the punctuation is much less evenly distributed than in that species, lastly the four anterior tibiæ are entirely black in *C. femoralis*, all the other described species differ either in the colour of the underside or legs and in their size; the male of the present insect has the first joint of the anterior tarsi elongate and rather thickened.

Cynorta flavilabris n. sp.

Metallic green or æneous, the antennæ, labrum and the legs, fulvous, thorax bifoveolate, impunctate, elytra finely punctured, the interstices slightly rugose.

Length 1 1/2 line.

Head impunctate, metallic green, frontal elevations strongly raised, transverse, clypeus in shape of narrow ridges, the anterior ones of which are deeply emarginate at the middle, labrum and palpi fulvous, antennæ rather long and robust, fulvous, the third joint double the length of the second, but half the length of the fourth joint, terminal joints shorter and rather thickened, thorax not longer than broad, subquadrate, the sides slightly constricted at the base, nearly straight. the disc impunctate, deeply bifoveolate, metallic green, elytra closely and finely punctured, the interstices slightly wrinkled or rugose, below metallic greenish, legs fulvous, the tibiæ mucronate, the metatarsus of the posterior legs, scarcely longer than the second joint, anterior coxal cavities closed.

Hab. Kanara, S. Bombay.

This small species resembles greatly several of its allies in size and general coloration; it is closely allied to *C. parvula* Jac., *C. subænea* Jac. and *C. granulata* Jac., from the first named, it is distinguished by the colour of the head and thorax and by the robust antennæ, from the second, by the colour of the antennæ, labrum and legs and from *C. granulata* by the colour of the thorax below and the differently sculptured elytra.

DORYSCUS TESTACEUS Jac.

Of this highly interesting species, a single specimen was obtained by Mr Andrewes at Kanara; I have also received some specimens from Sumatra obtained by Sign. Modigliani. The species is extremely variable in regard to coloration, scarcely two specimens being alike, the Kanara one has the elytra entirely fuscous, in some they are testaceous or margined with blackish. The type was described by me from Ceylon, in the description of the posterior claws, I stated at that time, that the latter were united at the base but divided at the extreme apex ; a close examination has now proved to me, that the claws must be moveable, as they are sometimes widely apart or so closely approached as to look joined, the apex only being divided ; in reallity the claws are simple but of great length and strongly curved, while the anterior claws are of normal size and appendiculate.

AGELOPSIS n. gen.

Body elongate, smooth, antennæ filiform, the first joint much thickened, the second short, the third, one half shorter than the fourth, this and the following joints very elongate, thorax subquadrate, transversely sulcate near the base, elytra irregularly punctured, their epipleuræ continued below the middle, legs slender, tibiæ unarmed, the metatarsus of the posterior legs as long as the following two joints together, claws appendiculate, prosternum not visible between the coxæ, the anterior coxal cavities closed.

The genus, proposed here seems allied to *Konbirella* Duviv. likewise from Bengal, to which I would have referred the present species, but the author describes the thorax as one third longer than broad, the tibiæ as mucronate and the anterior coxal cavities as open, neither is the case with the insect before me, which in other respect agrees singularly with Duvivier's description which I cannot assume as being erroneous in the above particulars.

Agelopsis caeruleus n. sp.

Entirely dark metallic blue, antennæ black, as long as the body, thorax impunctate, elytra distinctly and rather closely punctured.
Length 2 lines.

Head impunctate, broad, transversely grooved between the antennæ, frontal tubercles broadly trigonate, nearly contiguous, carina acute, clypeus narrowly transverse, labrum nearly black, palpi rather robust, antennæ extending to the end of the elytra, black, pubescent, the first joint smooth, metallic blue, strongly thickened, the fourth and following joints very elongate, thorax not longer than broad, the sides narrowed at the base, straight anteriorly, with a narrow margin, anterior angles slightly thickened but not produced, the surface entirely impunctate, with a rather broad transverse sulcus near the base, scutellum black, broad, elytra much broader at the base, than the thorax, distinctly but not very closely punctured, the punctures somewhat regularly arranged, underside and legs metallic dark blue like the upper surface, the apex of the tibiæ and the tarsi closely covered with yellowish pubescence.

Hab. Bengal (Konbir). My collection.

ADDENDA.

Gynandrophthalma orientalis n. sp.

Black. the basal joints of the antennæ and the base of the anterior tibiæ fulvous, thorax flavous, nearly impunctate, elytra strongly and closely punctured, dark blue, the apex flavous.

Length 1 line.

Head bluish-black, finely and sparingly punctured, not transversely depressed, the clypeus not separated from the face, labrum and palpi obscure fulvous, antennæ fuscous or black, the lower two or three joints fulvous, the second and third very small, the terminal joints transverse, thorax nearly three times broader than long. the sides nearly straight, the posterior angles rounded, the basal margin broadly truncate at the middle, scarcely produced, preceded by a very narrow transverse groove, the surface with a few minute punctures, flavous, scutellum broad, piceous, elytra very closely and distinctly punctured, the interstices finely rugose or wrinkled, the apex with a bright flavous spot, underside and legs black. finely pubescent, the base of the anterior femora more or less fulvous, the first joint of their tarsi very elongate, the metatarsus of the posterior legs as long as the following two joints together.

Hab. Belgaum.

A small sized species somewhat resembling *G. Raffrayi* and *G. collaris* of Europe in its coloration but differing in that of the elytra or the thorax respectively.

Nodostoma brunneum n. sp.

Dark fulvous, the terminal joints of the antennæ black, thorax transverse, the sides strongly dentate near the base, strongly punctate-striate.

Length 1 3/4-2 lines.

Head strongly but not very closely punctured in the male except on the clypeus, the latter not separated from the face, antennæ extending to the middle of the elytra, black, the lower four joints fulvous, all the joints slender, excepting the basal two, thorax strongly transverse, the sides oblique, forming a strong tooth near the base, the surface closely impressed with deep round punctures and the usual anterior transverse sulcus, elytra with the basal portion raised and impunctate, the shoulders acute and prominent, the disc regularly and strongly punctate striate, the punctures finer towards the apex, underside and legs impunctate, the posterior femora with a small tooth, prosternum broader than long, flancs of the thorax strongly and closely punctured.

Hab. Ihrawaddy.

One of the larger species and closely allied to *N. puncticolle* Lefèv. (nec Weise) but of entirely fulvous colour and the thorax less deeply and closely punctured; in *N. puncticolle* of which I possess a typical specimen, the punctures are nearly confluent at the sides, which is not the case here, the raised basal portion of the elytra is also impunctate in the present insect, in the allied species, it is strongly punctured; the five specimens before me show no variation except in size.

Colasposoma prosternale n. sp.

Metallic green, the antennæ, labrum and the legs dark fulvous, thorax very closely punctured, the sides strongly rounded, elytra rather closely and regularly punctured at the suture, the sides more strongly punctate, prosternum thickly pubescent.

Mas. Thorax deeply impressed behind the anterior margin.

Length 2 lines.

Head very finely punctured, the punctures moderately closely placed, labrum and antennæ fulvous, thorax strongly transversely convex, the sides greatly rounded, narrowly margined, the surface closely, finely and evenly punctured throughout, with a short but deep transverse impression at the middle, behind the anterior margin, scutellum sparingly punctured, elytra with a very slight depression below the base, more strongly punctured at the sides, than towards the suture, the interstices slightly rugose at the former place, breast slightly metallic green, the abdomen nearly black, prosternum densely clothed with greyish pubescence, the male organ strongly curved, gradually narrowed and pointed at the apex.

Hab. Ihrawaddy.

There are many closely allied and variable Eastern species of *Colasposoma*, difficult to separate and of which many specimens are necessary for a satisfactory recognition; the present species seems very closely allied to *C. asperatum* Lefèv. of which I possess a typical specimen, but I cannot identify it with the latter, as the antennæ and the legs are dark fulvous, not metallic green, the head and thorax is less closely punctured and the prosternum is thickly clothed with pubescence, which does not permit any sculpturing to be seen; this is the case in the ten or more specimens before me; the prosternum in *C. asperatum* is smooth and strongly punctured; in the female of the present insect, the thorax shows scarcely any transverse groove, but in the male, the latter is very strongly marked, the elytral rugosities in the female are as usual, very distinct at the sides, but not anything so strong or tuberculate as in *C. asperatum*.

Pseudocolaspis discoidalis n. sp.

Metallic greenish-æneous, pubescent, the basal joints of the antennæ and the legs more or less fulvous, thorax finely and closely punctured, elytra more strongly punctured, the sides and apex pale fulvous, the base and suture metallic greenish.

Length 1 1/2 line.

Head closely punctured and slightly rugose, æneous, the epistome not separated from the face, bounded laterally by a narrow ridge, antennæ extending to the base of the thorax, fulvous; the first and second joint thickened, nearly equal, terminal joints distincly dilated, not longer than broad, thorax about as long as broad, gradually widened at the middle, the surface finely and not very closely punctured, cupreous or æneous, clothed with grey pubescence; scutellum subquadrate, its apex truncate, elytra wider at the base than the thorax, more closely and rather more strongly punctured, the punctures arranged in very closely approached irregular rows, rather sparingly pubescent like the thorax, the sides and apex fulvous, the disc, in shape of a triangular patch, gradually narrowed and pointed along the suture, greenish æneous, underside also metallic greenish, legs fulvous, the tarsi piceous, prosternum broadly subquadrate, sparingly punctured, femora with a very small tooth.

North West Provinces.

I am not acquainted with any species of this genus, possessing similarly coloured elytra, there are several specimens before me which show no difference in this respect; in all, the metallic discoïdal patch commences broadly at the base and gets gradually narrowed towards the apex, which it does not quite reach, the pubescence of the elytra is stiff and arranged more regularly near the apex; in some specimens, the apical joints of the antennæ are nearly black.